暢銷修訂版 | English for International Trade: Speaking and Writing

倍斯特出版事業有限公司
Best Publishing Ltd.

國貿 英語說寫 一本通！

施美怡◎著

在全世界成功談生意＝
優秀英語對話＋專業英語書信
接電話，手忙腳亂
……，腦汁榨乾？

晉升專業國貿人

流程全方位：從開發業務到保險賠償
能力全方位：買方＋賣方 對話＋書信 知識＋經驗
適合各國貿系所、貿易公司、國外業務和船務實務
自學讓你提升職場英語競爭力！

全面提升英語力

・搞懂國貿流程：對客戶、船公司、
  保險公司、開狀銀行…
・精選商業和辦公室一定用的到的
  【關鍵字彙】和【關鍵句型】

在現今全球化的經濟市場中，英文已不再是個口號，而是職場中不可或缺的基本條件之一，出國深造是多數立志從事國貿行業或外文相關行業所嚮往的，然而並非所有人都能負擔的起龐大的留學費用，而國內教育所提供的多屬理論且大於實用。

本書所提供的是作者在國際貿易領域十多年的實務經驗所碰到的各種情境，以國際貿易中兩大主角「買方（進口商）」及「賣方（出口商）」為角度切入，以情境對話帶入主題，連結實用字彙及句型，而後導入國貿人員幾乎天天需要面對，卻也是國貿新鮮人最棘手的「英文書信」，由淺入深，也沒有艱深的字彙、枯燥的文法，及長篇的文章，並在【知識補給】及【職場經驗談】單元提供國貿相關知識及分享實務經驗，希望能讓讀者輕鬆學、愉快學。

誰說「自然而然學英語」一定要花大把鈔票出國深造或聘請外師一對一學會話，只要用心，相信自己，萬事皆不難。 "Sometimes the hardest thing and the right thing are the same!" 去做，就對了！

施美怡

台灣擁有絕佳的國際貿易地理位置，想當然爾成為支持台灣經濟的重要支柱。做好一個國貿人，除了需要熟悉國貿知識和累積實務的經驗，優秀的外語能力更是核心競爭力。隨著現今通訊軟體的功能日益強大，商用書信是必備的溝通模式外，業務們視訊會議和外地出差的機會明顯變多了，直接與國外客戶對話溝通的機會也大幅增加了。

《國貿英語說寫一本通暢銷修訂版》即以國貿中的最主要的溝通方式—書信寫作和口語溝通為重點，更新國貿法規和資訊外，重整 76 個國貿實務【情境對話】、【職場補給】、【職場經驗談】和【英文書信這樣寫】單元，幫助讀者以另外一種活潑的方式搞懂國貿流程—從開發業務到賠償問題。

最後，希望各位讀者讀完此書後，能勇敢開口說，面對客戶，掌握談判關鍵，成功解決問題。不管是國貿老手還是國貿新鮮人，都能加強英文能力和國貿專業知識，讓您輕鬆晉升專業國貿人，幫助各位在國貿職場上一路過關斬將。

倍斯特編輯部

CONTENTS

目錄

Chapter 1　開發業務和價格條件

Chapter 2 付款條件和保險條件

交貨條件 —— 運輸

Chapter 4　買賣/運輸/保險賠償

Chapter 1

開發業務和價格條件

Development of Business and Price Terms

產品目錄索取和寄送
Request and Delivery of Catalogue

國貿關鍵字 | 產品目錄 |

　　產品目錄為商業中最常見的行銷手法之一，以得知賣方詳細產品資訊。產品目錄為開發業務的開端，因此扮演舉足輕重的角色，除了是否滿意價格和產品，在書信中索取及寄發產品目錄的用字也可能關係著商業關係可否建立。

　　一般來說，賣方通常不會拒絕索取產品目錄者，為了避免同業藉此竊取產品資訊，賣方也可以先做初步商業調查，瞭解對方公司背景。正式進行交易時，有可能會進行正式的信用調查。

情境說明

The buyer contacts with the seller to request the catalogue to have further product information.

買方公司聯繫賣方公司索取產品目錄和進一步的產品資訊。

角色介紹

買方 | Buyer: B, ABC Co., Ltd.

賣方 | Seller: S, Best International Trade Corp.

情境對話

S: Best Corp. This is Mary. How may I help you?

S: 倍斯特公司您好！我是瑪莉，請問需要什麼協助嗎？

B: Hi! This is Tom Smith calling from ABC Co., Ltd. I'd like to know about your product details.

B: 您好！我是ABC公司的湯姆 史密斯，我想要瞭解您公司產品的明細。

S: Please hold on. I'll transfer the line to our product department.

S: 請稍等一下，我幫您轉接我們的產品部門。

S: Hi! This is Tony Yang, the Product Manager of Best Corp.

S: 您好！我是倍斯特公司的產品經理湯尼 楊。

B: Hi! This is Tom Smith calling from ABC Co., Ltd. I have seen the advertisement for your products. I'd like to have a list of your valves.

B: 您好! 我是ABC公司的湯姆史密斯。我有看到您們公司產品的廣告，我想要一份您們公司閥門的產品目錄。

S: Thanks for your attention to our products, but I am sorry that the catalogue is under revision. I will send you one once the updated version is available.

S: 感謝您關注我們的產品，但很抱歉，產品目錄正在修訂中，新版推出後，我就會寄給您。

B: Please send the catalogue together with the price list.

B: 請您也將價格表連同目錄一起寄給我。

S: No problem. I will send you the documents as requested once theyre ready.

S: 沒問題，您所需的文件一準備好之後，我就會寄給您。

B: Very appreciate. I will give you our address by email later.

B: 十分感激！稍後我會以電子郵件通知您我們的地址。

11

情境說明

The seller Best International Trade Corp. informs the buyer ABC Co. Ltd about the delivery of the requested catalogue and asks them to confirm back on receipt of the catalogue.

賣方公司通知買方公司已寄出產品目錄並請對方收到目錄後進行確認。

角色介紹

買方｜Buyer: B, ABC Co., Ltd.

賣方｜Seller: S, Best International Trade Corp.

情境對話

S: I'm calling <u>to inform you that</u> we forwarded to you the requested catalogue by express this morning.

S：撥打此通電話是要通知您我們已在今日上午以快遞寄出我們的產品目錄給您。

B: Great. When can I expect to receive it?

B：太好了。預計何時可我可以收到產品目錄？

S: The parcel will arrive at your office by next Monday. I'll email you the tracking number later.

S：包裹會在下週一前送到您公司，稍後我會將快遞提單號碼電郵給您。

S: <u>Please confirm back</u> upon receipt of the catalogue.

S：請您在收到型錄後回覆確認一聲。

B: By the way, could you offer some samples of your valve?

B：順道一提，是否可提供一些您們的閥門樣品呢？

12

S: Sure, after studying our catalogue. please just advise us the item number.

S：沒問題。等您看過我們的型錄後再請告訴我們品號即可。

B: Thanks again.

B：再次感謝。

S: We hope you will be satisfied with our products.

S：希望您會滿意我司的產品。

關鍵字彙

◎ **product** *n.* [`prɑdəkt] 產品

同義詞：commodity, merchandise, good

相關詞：by-product 副產品

◎ **advertisement** *n.* [͵ædvə`taɪzmənt] 廣告

同義詞：commercial

相關詞：newspaper advertisement 報紙廣告；classified advertisement 分類廣告

◎ **catalogue** *n.* [`kætələg] 目錄（＝（美）catalog）

同義詞：brochure, list

相關詞：catalogue marketing 目錄行銷

◎ **detail** *n.* [`ditel] 詳細

相關詞：price details 報價明細；inventory details 庫存明細；in detail 詳細地

◎ **under revision** *ph.* [`ʌndə rɪ`vɪʒən] 改版

同義詞：under change, under modification, under amendment, under editing

解　析：常用於說明文件、產品型錄、產品設計圖等的版本修訂

13

updated version *ph.* [ʌpˋdetɪˋvɝʒən] 最新版本

同義詞：the newest version, the latest version, the most recent rersion

解　析：常用於說明文件、產品型錄、產品設計圖等最新發行的版本

inform *v.* [ɪnˋfɔrm] 通知

同義詞：tell, advise, notify, report

相關詞：inform...about 使⋯知道；inform...of 使⋯知道

forward *v.* [ˋfɔrwɚd] 運送

同義詞：send, dispatch, pass, deliver

相關詞：look forward to 期待

arrive *v.* [əˋraɪv] 抵達

同義詞：come, reach, get to

相關詞：arrive at / in 到達

offer *v.* [ˋɔfɚ] 提供

同義詞：supply, provide, submit

相關詞：firm offer 確認價；special offer 特價

upon receipt of Sth. *ph.* 收到某物時

同義詞：on receipt of Sth.

解　析：常用於說明收到產品型錄、報價單、出貨單等商業相關文件

item number *ph.* 品號

同義詞：part number

解　析：常用於說明單一產品的品號，以利區分個別差異產品

關鍵句型

I'd like to know about sth.　我想要瞭解關於某事

例句說明：

- **I'd like to know** about your merchandise.
  我想要瞭解貴司的產品訊息。
- **I'd like to know** about your payment term.
  我想要瞭解貴司的付款條件。

I am sorry for + 名詞片語 或 **that** + 子句　對於...感到抱歉

例句說明：

- **I am sorry for** the late delivery.
  很抱歉交貨有所延遲。

Please confirm back.　請回覆確認

例句說明：

- **Please confirm back** once the shipment is released.
  待出貨放行後，還請回覆確認。
- **Please confirm back** by mail once the sample is approved.
  等樣品一核準後，還請回函確認。

inform Sb. about Sth. + 名詞片語 或 **that** + 子句　通知某人某事

例句說明：

- **We're writing to inform you about** the item numbers of the products of our interest.
- **We're writing to inform you that** that we're interesting in the following items.
  通知您我們有興趣的產品（品號）。

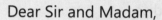

Request of Catalogue 索取產品目錄

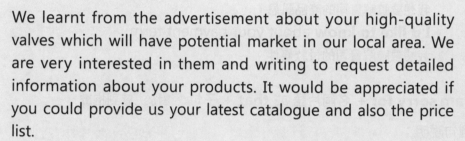

Dear Sir and Madam,

We learnt from the advertisement about your high-quality valves which will have potential market in our local area. We are very interested in them and writing to request detailed information about your products. It would be appreciated if you could provide us your latest catalogue and also the price list.

Looking forward to your prompt response.

Sincerely yours,
Tom Smith

─ 中文翻譯 ─

您好，

我們從廣告中得知您公司有高品質的閥門產品，這在我們當地有潛在的市場，我們很有感興趣，在此請求您提供詳細的產品訊息。如您能提供最新的產品目錄及價格表，我們將十分感激。

期待您早日回覆。

湯姆 史密斯 敬啟

1 開發業務和價格條件

2

3

4

Delivery of Catalogue 寄送產品目錄

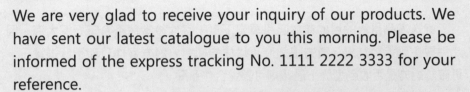

Dear Mr. Smith,

We are very glad to receive your inquiry of our products. We have sent our latest catalogue to you this morning. Please be informed of the express tracking No. 1111 2222 3333 for your reference.

The catalogue includes all models of valves we produce and their prices list for your study. We are very confident that the high-quality and reasonable prices of our products are more competitive than other suppliers, and will be very popular with your local customers. We believe you will be satisfied with our products and look forward to establishing business relationship with you.

Please feel free to contact us if you have any queries.

Sincerely yours,
Tony Yang

－ 中文翻譯 －

史密斯 先生 您好；

非常開心收到貴司詢問我司產品的來信。我司已於今日上午把最新的產品目錄寄給您。茲通知快遞提單號碼為 1111 2222 3333，供您參考。

產品目錄包含我司所生產的所有閥門型號及價格表供您檢閱。非常有信心我司高品質及合理之價格比其他供應商更具競爭力，並將深受您當地客戶的青睞。深信貴司將對我司產品感到滿意，我司期待與貴司建立合作關係。

如有任何需求，請隨時與我司聯繫。

湯尼 楊 敬啟

寄發產品目錄後之追蹤（符合或不符合買方需求）

Follow-up after Catalogue Delivery (Conforming or Not conforming to Buyer's Demand)

國貿關鍵字 | 寄發產品目錄 |

　　寄送產品目錄的目的在於吸引買方下單，寄件後當然不希望石沉大海，因此需要主動追蹤結果。賣方追蹤時可以先告知對方對方寄件日和預計送達日，再確認對方是否收到型錄，最後則可表達合作意願。

　　國際快遞運送時間以台灣至歐洲為例通常不逾7天，再加上給予對方檢視目錄的時間，因此在寄出產品目錄後的一至兩週內即可以向對方做第一次的追蹤確認。

情境說明

After sending out catalogues, Best Corp. the seller tracks the results of reviewing product catalogue, ABC Co. the buyer confirms the products meet their needs.

在寄送產品目錄後，賣方公司追蹤買方公司的回覆，買方公司確認其產品符合公司需求。

角色介紹

買方 | Buyer: B, ABC Co., Ltd.

賣方 | Seller: S, Best International Trade Corp.

情境對話

S: Hi! Tom. This is Tony at Best Corp. I want to <u>confirm</u> if you have received our catalogue sent to you last week.

S：湯姆 您好！我是倍斯特公司的湯尼。我想確認您是否已經收到我司寄給您的產品目錄。

B: The catalogue was received this morning. Really appreciate your prompt delivery.

B：今天早上已經收到目錄了，非常感謝您如此快速的安排寄送事宜。

S: I wonder Whether you have the chance to browse through the catalogue?

S：您是否已有機會翻閱目錄了呢？

B: Yes, we read the catalogue carefully and found it excludes 3/4" ball valve we requested.

B：是的，我已經仔細看過目錄了，並且發現目錄中缺少了我司所需求的3/4英吋規格的球閥。

S: Oh no! Please accept our apology.

S：哎呀！請接受我們的歉意。

B: It's OK. Please send the missing one as soon as you can.

B：沒關係。請儘速寄出遺漏的部分。

S: I will send it off by International Priority today.

S：今天我會安排以國際優先速遞寄出。

B: Great. I will give you a definite answer after reviewing all product information.

B：太好了。檢視所有產品資料後，我會提供您明確的回覆。

S: Sorry again for our oversight. If there's further need, just drop me a message or send me an email.

S：針對此次疏失，我再次致歉！如果有進一步需要，儘管傳簡訊或寄郵件給我。

B: I will. Bye now.

B：我會的，那麼再見了。

情境說明

After sending out catalogues, Best Corp. the seller tracks the results of reviewing product catalogue, ABC Co. the buyer confirms the products doesn't meet their needs.

在寄送產品目錄後，賣方公司追蹤買方公司的回覆，買方公司確認其產品不符合公司需求。

角色介紹

買方｜Buyer: B, ABC Co., Ltd.

賣方｜Seller: S, Best International Trade Corp.

情境對話

B: This is Tom Smith.

B：我是湯姆 史密斯。

S: Hi ! Tom. It's Tony from Best Corp.

S：您好！湯姆。我是倍斯特公司的湯尼。

B: Hello, Tony. I've been meaning to get back to you all the week. How are you doing?

B：您好！湯尼。整個星期我一直想要回電給您，最近好嗎？

S: Not bad. I'm calling to follow up on the catalogue sent to you last week.

S：還不賴！打給您是為了追蹤上週寄給您的產品目錄事。

B: I did get it and went through all pages. Unfortunately, the products can't completely fit our demand. Sorry about that.

B：我確實收到了，也看完了。但不幸的是貴司的產品無法完全符合我司的需求，實在抱歉。

S: Oh! That's OK. But we'd appreciate it very much if you could introduce some potential buyers to us.

S：喔！沒關係，但如果您能引薦一些潛在客戶給我們，我們將非常感激。

B: Sure.

B：沒問題。

S: I'm still hoping for another opportunity to serve you. So if you need any requirement in the future, please <u>never hesitate</u> to ring me up.

S：仍然希望有其它機會能為您服務。所以如果未來貴司有任何需求，請儘管打電話給我。

B: I'll be sure to let you know.

B：我一定會告訴您。

關鍵字彙

⊘ **confirm** *v.* [kən`fɝm] 確認
同義詞：verify, prove, settle
相關詞：confirmed L/C 保兌信用狀

⊘ **receive** *v.* [rɪ`siv] 收到
同義詞：obtain, accept, gain, take, get in
相關詞：receive feedback 收到反饋；receive bonuses 獲得獎金

⊘ **oversight** *n.* [`ovəˌsaɪt] 疏忽
同義詞：slip, negligence, omission, error
相關詞：gross oversight 重大疏失

⊘ **send off** *ph.* 郵寄
同義詞：send away, dispatch, post

browse through *ph.* 翻閱、瀏覽

同義詞：glance trough

解　析：隨意翻閱或瀏覽文件、書籍、期刊等

demand *n.* [dɪ`mænd] 需求

同義詞：need, requirement

相關詞：demand bill 即期匯票或支票；supply and demand 供需關係

potential *a.* [pə`tɛnʃəl] 潛在

同義詞：possible, likely, hidden

相關詞：commercial potential 商機潛力；potential consumers 潛在消費者

opportunity *n.* [ˌɑpə`tjunətɪ] 機會

同義詞：chance, possibility

相關詞：opportunity cost 機會成本；opportunity only knocks once 機不可失

hesitate *v.* [`hɛzəˌtet] 猶豫

同義詞：boggle, hover, vibrate, pause

相關詞：hesitater 猶豫不決的人

get back to Sb. *ph.* 回電某人

同義詞：call Sb. back, wire back, return one's call

相關詞：get back 回來、恢復、找回

follow up *ph.* 持續追蹤

同義詞：keep track of

相關詞：follow-up system 追蹤系統

關鍵句型

I want to confirm ... 我想確認

例句說明：

- **I want to confirm** if all the parts are available.
  我想確認是否所有產品都有現貨。
- **I want to confirm** my flight reservation.
  我想確認我預定的班機。

Please accept Sb.'s apologies. 請接受某人的歉意

例句說明：

- **Please accept my apology for** my oversight.
  請原諒我的疏失。
- **Please accept our apology for** any inconvenience we have caused.
  若有不便，敬請見諒。

have been meaning to ... 一直⋯

例句說明：

- Tom and Tony **have been meaning to** get in touch with each other.
  湯姆及湯尼一直保持聯絡。

Never hesitate to ... 不要猶豫

例句說明：

- In case you need something, please **never hesitate to** ask me.
  如果你需要什麼，別客氣請儘管問我。

英文書信這樣寫

Follow-up after Catalogue Delivery 寄發型錄後之追蹤

Dear Tom,

I am writing to ask if you received our catalogue sent to you last week per your request. One week has passed, but no response has been received. Just to be sure, I am enclosing a copy of our catalogue for your reference. We would be grateful if you could confirm receipt of it by return.

We look forward to hearing from you soon.

Sincerely yours,
Tony Yang

– 中文翻譯 –

湯姆 您好：

在此詢問貴司是否有收到上週我司依貴司要求所寄出之產品目錄。已過了一週，我司仍未收到任何回覆。為了保險起見，我在此附上目錄一份供您參考。如貴司能回覆確認收到，我司將不勝感激。

期待您的儘速回覆。

湯尼 楊 敬啟

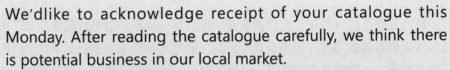

Reply after Receive the Catalogue 收到型錄後之回覆

Dear Tony,

We'dlike to acknowledge receipt of your catalogue this Monday. After reading the catalogue carefully, we think there is potential business in our local market.

Please offer the quotation sheet as well as payment method for 3/4" ball valve. We will place a trial order firstly.

Looking forward to establishing long-term cooperation between us soon.

Sincerely yours,
Tom Smith

– 中文翻譯 –

湯尼 您好：

有此通知您，我司已在本週一收到你們的型錄。仔細看過目錄後，我司認為貴司產品在我們當地市場有潛在的商機。

煩請提供3/4英吋球閥的報價單及付款方式，我司將先下一批試訂單。

期待很快能與貴司建立長期合作關係。

湯姆 史密斯 敬啟

索取樣品和客戶聯繫

Request of Sample and Customer Connection

國貿關鍵字 | 索取樣品 |

買方看過產品目錄後,可以要求賣方提供部分樣品,這是檢視樣品和了解產品性能最直接的方式,但考量其他因素,賣方可以僅提供部分品項和另外收取樣品費用。索取樣品告知所需之型號、顏色、材質和規格等,或直接請賣方提供其最暢銷的款式。

情境說明

ABC Co. the buyer confirms the products of Best Corp. the seller fit their needs, and therefore asks to provide samples for further review.

買方公司確認賣方公司的產品符合需求,因此索取樣品以做進一步檢視。

角色介紹

買方 | Buyer: B, ABC Co., Ltd.

賣方 | Seller: S, Best International Trade Corp.

情境對話

B: Hello. This is Tom Smith at ABC Co.

B:您好!我是ABC公司的湯姆‧史密斯。

S: Hi. Tom. How have you been lately?

S:您好!湯姆。近來好嗎?

B: Not bad. Now I have received the right catalogue and it's very clear. I'm calling to request some samples for our factory in California.

B：還不錯。我現在收到正確的目錄了且內容非常清楚。我打電話來替我們加州的工廠索取一些樣品。

S: Which of our items are you interested in?

S：您對哪個品項感興趣呢？

B: We'd like to have P/N 0001 and 0002. Will there be a charge for the samples?

B：我想要產品編號 0001 及 0002 的產品。請問是否收取樣品費用？

S: We can provide you as many as two free samples of each item. Please give me the plant address and I'll have them shipped out at your request tomorrow.

S：我們最多可提供每個品項兩個免費樣品。請提供貴司的工廠住址，我會應您的要求在明天寄出樣品。

B: That's great. I will e-mail it to you before punching out.

B：那太好了！下班前我會將住址 e-mail 給您。

S: I'll send you a response after getting the e-mail.

S：收到您的 email 後我會回覆您。

B: Thank you once again. Talk to you soon.

B：再次感謝，以後再聊。

情境說明

In response to business expansion, Best Corp. the seller demand ABC Co. the buyer to recommend customers.

為了業務擴展，賣方公司請求買方公司推薦客戶。

角色介紹

買方 | Buyer: B, ABC Co., Ltd.

賣方 | Seller: S, Best International Trade Corp.

情境對話

S: As you know, the sales of our products keep growing. Our goal in the next quarter is to enter into EU market.

S：就您所知道的，我們的產品銷售量持續成長，我們下一季的目標是進軍歐盟市場

B: Glad to hear that.

B：很高興聽到這個消息。

S: I'm wondering if you could introduce some potential clients to us.

S：不知道您能否為我們引薦一些潛在客戶？

B: I happen to know that one of our business partners is looking for supplier of industrial valves. We have cooperated with this company for many years. I think there is a great cooperative opportunity for you.

B：我剛好知道我們的其中一位合作夥伴正在尋找工業閥門的供應商，我們和這家公司已合作多年，我想這對您來說是一個很好的合作機會。

S: That's great!

S：太好了！

B: I'll send you the contact information about the customer later.

B：稍後我會將這個客戶的聯絡資訊寄給你。

S: I want to <u>thank you again for</u> your assistance with this.

S：我想再次感謝您在這件事情上的協助。

B: That's all right. I'm glad that I can give you a hand.

B：不客氣，很高興能幫上忙。

關鍵字彙

⊘ **sample** *n.* [ˋsæmp!] 樣品
同義詞：specimen, example
相關詞：sample size 樣本量，floor sample 陳列商品

⊘ **factory** *n.* [ˋfæktərɪ] 工廠，製造商
同義詞：plant, works
相關詞：factory building 廠房，factory-made 工廠生產的

⊘ **response** *n.* [rɪˋspɑns] 回覆
同義詞：answer, reply, feedback
相關詞：response time 回應時間

⊘ **ship** *v.* [ʃɪp] 郵寄、運送
同義詞：transport, send, dispatch
相關詞：ship out 送出、寄出，take ship 上船

⊘ **charge for Sth.** *ph.* 為某物索價
同義詞：rate, ask as a price
解　析：常用於說明商業行為中收取相關費用，如樣品費、文件費、運費…等

⊘ **punch out** *ph.* 下班

同義詞：knock off, clock out

解　析：打卡離開，意指下班

⊘ **goal** *n.* [gol] 目標

同義詞：destination, objective, target

相關詞：goal orientation 目標取向，goal setting 目標設定

⊘ **partner** *n.* [`pɑrtnɚ] 夥伴

同義詞：collaborator, cooperator

相關詞：partnership 合夥關係；sleeping partner 不參與實際業務的股東

⊘ **supplier** *n.* [sə`plaɪɚ] 供應商

同義詞：provider

相關詞：suppliers' credit ratings 供應商的信用評等

⊘ **cooperate with** Sb. *ph.* 與某人合作

同義詞：collaborate with, play along with, go along with

相關詞：cooperate with each other 互相合作

⊘ **keep growing** *ph.* 持續成長

同義詞：continue to grow, obtain sustainable growth

相關詞：the losses keep growing 損失持續增加

⊘ **give Sb. a hand** *ph.* 協助某人

同義詞：assist, help, do Sb. a favor,

相關詞：give me a hand with the parcel 幫我拿一下包裹

關鍵句型

at one's request　應某人要求

例句說明：

· She came **at my request**.
她應我的請求而來。
· **At your request** we offer you a special price.
應您的要求，我們提供一個優惠價。

be interested in Sth.　對某物感興趣

例句說明：

· He's not interested in attending provincial exhibitions.
他對參加地方展不感興趣。
· Since when have you been interested in international trade?
你從什麼時候開始對國際貿易感興趣？

be wondering if　不知是否

例句說明：

· **I am wondering if** we can arrange a meeting to discuss the new project.
不知我們是否可以安排一次會議，討論新專案。
· **I am wondering if** you can give me a hand with the parcel.
不知你是否能幫我拿一下包裹。

thank Sb. for Sth.　感謝某人做某事

例句說明：

· **We thank you for** the special price you offered us.
感謝貴司提供優惠價。

1 開發業務和價格條件

2

3

4

31

英文書信這樣寫

索取樣品 **Request of Sample**

Dear Tony,

Many thanks for the catalogue sent to us last week. We are very pleased with your products and would like to request some samples of P/N 0001 and 0002. We plan to place an initial order after further reviewing the sample.

Please advise if you'd charge for the cost of the samples. If so, we'll place a sample order to you.

Your prompt reply will be greatly appreciated.

Sincerely yours,
Tom Smith

– 中文翻譯 –

湯尼 您好：

十分感激您上週寄給我司產品目錄。我們非常滿意貴司的產品，想跟您索取編號0001及0002的樣品，我們預計檢視樣品後下首批訂單。

請告知貴司是否須收取樣品費。如是，我們將會下樣品訂單。

您的即時回覆將不勝感激。

湯姆 史密斯 敬啟

需求引薦客戶 Request of Customer Recommendation

Dear Tom,

Thank you for the continued support to us.

As you know, our company is expanding our business oversea. We would appreciate if you could kindly recommend some potential customers to us.

Thank you in advance for your assistance.

Sincerely yours,
Tony Yang

— 中文翻譯 —

湯姆 您好：

感謝您對我司一直以來的支持。

如您所知，我司正在擴展海外業務。如您能引薦一些潛在客戶給我們，我司將不勝感激。

先感謝您的幫忙與協助。

湯尼 楊 敬啟

職場經驗談

索取樣品以小批量為主，通常為一至數十件不等，因此多會選擇快遞運輸方式。寄件時，即使外包裝已特別註明不可重摔、小心輕放等字樣，但難保快遞員會妥善處理，所以堅固內外包裝極為重要，例如使用內盒、泡棉、氣泡袋、隔板，以避免運輸過程中相互碰撞。但切勿重重包裹外盒，例如以多層膠帶包纏將造成拆解困難，也會造成收件者的困擾。

詢價報價
Inquiry & Quotation

國貿關鍵字 ｜報價｜

　　報價給客戶必須謹慎，尤其是牽涉到價格及付款條件。依公司與客戶的合作關係來決定彼此的合作模式和付款條件。新客戶需在收到訂單確認書後，立即付清款項；舊客戶則享有較寬鬆的付款條件。此外，報價過程一定要小心的，若提供不正確的報價，不僅公司專業度會被質疑，有時因訂貨數量大，甚至需要賠錢以示負責。

情境說明

The buyer accepts the payment terms of L/C by the seller..

買方公司同意賣方公司要求以信用狀為付款條件。

角色介紹
買方｜Buyer: B, ABC Co., Ltd.

賣方｜Seller: S, Best International Trade Corp.

情境對話

B: I want to place an order of your valve accessory #001. I'd like to go ahead and place an order for two hundred units.

B：我想向跟您下單訂購 #001 閥門配件。我想就先下兩百組。

S: We shall be pleased to enter your order at special price, of USD20 per unit. We usually don't grant discount for small quantities.

S：我們願意提供單價20美元的優惠價，通常對於小額訂單，我們是不提供折扣的。

B: Thanks! I'll <u>further talk to</u> my supervisor about it.

B：謝謝！我會再與主管討論這個價格。

S: As our stocks are running short, we would recommend you to place your order soon.

S：因為我們的現貨不多了，建議貴公司儘快下訂單。

B: Sure, I will <u>make sure to</u> get back to you in just a few days. Could you please also give me your formal quotation?

B：當然，我保證就在這幾天回覆您。請問您可以提供我正式的報價嗎？

S: No problem. I'll ensure to email it to you by 5:00PM today.

S：沒問題，我保證在今日下午五點 email 給您。

B: Great! Appreciate your help.

B：太好了！感謝您的幫忙。

情境說明

The buyer wants to place a special order; therefore, it contacts with the seller to request formal quotation.

買方公司欲下特殊訂單，因此要求賣方公司提供正式產品報價。

角色介紹

買方｜Buyer: B, ABC Co., Ltd.

賣方｜Seller: S, Best International Trade Corp.

情境對話

B: Please make an offer as per the inquiry sheet I sent you this morning and give us your best price.

B：請依據我今早寄給您的詢價單報價，並給我們最好的價格。

S: As you know, the price always depends on quantity.

S：您知道價格永遠取決於數量。

B: Actually, this is a sample order for exhibition preparation. We anticipate that the exhibition will bring profound economic benefits with a mass of order.

B：事實上，這是一筆做為參展準備的樣品訂單，我們期待展覽將帶來更大的經濟效益和大量的訂單。

S: In this case, we can make an extra 5% special discount.

S：如果是這樣，我們可以提供額外5% 的特別折扣。

B: Do you offer FOB or CIF prices?

B：您報的價格是離岸價或到岸價呢？

S: All prices are on FOB basis.

S：所有價格皆為離岸價。

B: We'd rather you quote CIF New York.

B：我們想請您提供紐約到岸價。

S: No problem. I'll work out the number and let you have our offer sheet tomorrow. Is there anything else you needed?

S：沒問題，我會核算後於明天給您報價單。請問還有其它需要嗎？

B: Yes, we are hoping the sample packaged with a double bubble bag. You may include the package cost to the piece price, if needed.

B：有的，我們希望樣品以雙層氣泡袋包裝，如果有需要計費，您可以將包裝成本計入產品單價中。

S: We could do that free of charge.

S：我們可以免費提供此包裝。

B: That's great! I really appreciate it.

B：太好了！十分感激。

關鍵字彙

⊘ **accessory** *n.* [æk`sɛsərɪ] 零件
同義詞：part, component
相關詞：accessory charges 額外費用；accessory equipment 輔助設備

⊘ **grant** *v.* [grænt] 授予
同義詞：give, award, bestow
相關詞：grant-in-aid 資助款；grant a favor 幫忙

⊘ **place an order** *ph.* 下單

同義詞：make an order, give an order, order

相關詞：accept order 接單

⊘ **be running short** *ph.* 逐漸短缺

同義詞：be running low, deficit

相關詞：overproduction 生產過剩

⊘ **depend on** *ph.* 視某事物而定

同義詞：rely on, count on, rest on

相關詞：depend on work experience 取決於工作經驗

⊘ **inquiry sheet** *ph.* 詢價單

同義詞：enquiry sheet, RFQ (request for quotation)

相關詞：inquiry period 調查期間

⊘ **offer sheet** *ph.* 報價單

同義詞：quotation sheet, quotation

解　析：價目表（price list）與報價單（offer sheet; quotation sheet）的不同之處在於
　　　　價目表為賣方用於詳列其所生產販賣產品的相關品項、規格、價格等，僅為參考文
　　　　件，不具要約效力，報價單則為賣方承諾可接受的價格與交易條件，屬於要約。

⊘ **package cost** *ph.* 包裝成本

同義詞：packing cost, packing charge, packaging cost

相關詞：pre-packaged（食品銷售前）預包裝的；packaging 包裝（業）

⊘ **piece price** *ph.* 單價

同義詞：unit price

相關詞：total price 總價；cost price 成本價

1 CHAPTER 開發業務和價格條件

2

3

4

關鍵句型

further talk to Sb. about Sth. 　與某人進一步談某事

例句說明：

- I **further talk to** the consignee **about** the shipping schedule.
  我進一步跟收貨人談論出貨計畫。
- My boss **further talked to** me **about** my performance.
  主管進一步跟我談我的業績。

Sth. always depends on ... 　某事物永遠取決於⋯

例句說明：

- The opportunities **always depend on** the previous work experience and qualifications.
  機會永遠取決於工作經歷和學歷。

Sb. anticipate that Sth. will bring ... 　期待某物帶來⋯

例句說明：

- The government **anticipate that** the new policy **will bring** the economic recovery.
  政府期待新政策帶來經濟復甦。

英文書信這樣寫

Inquiry 詢價

Dear Tony,

We hereby acknowledge receipt of the sample you sent to us last week and find your product quality satisfactory. We'd like to inquire about the piece price of your P/N 0007 and 0008 as well as payment terms.

We should be obliged by your early reply.

Sincerely yours,
Tom Smith

– 中文翻譯 –

湯尼 您好：

在此通知已收到貴司上週寄來的樣品，我司相當滿意您的產品品質，想詢問產品件號 0007 及 0008 之單價及付款條件。

如貴司能早日回覆，我司將不勝感激。

湯姆 史密斯 敬啟

Quotation 報價

Dear Tom,

Thanks for your inquiry about our products. The quotation as requested is as follows:

P/N 0007   USD4.50 / pc
P/N 0008   USD5.00 / pc

Please refer to the attached quotation sheet listing and MCQ payment terms and MOQ.

Please contact us any time if you have any further question.

Sincerely yours,
Tony Yang

2

3

4

- 中文翻譯 -

湯姆 您好:

感謝貴司對我司產品的詢問。依據貴司要求提供報價如下:
P/N 0007   美金 $4.50 / 件
P/N 0008   美金 $5.00 / 件
請參考附件報價單所列最低訂購量要求及付款條件。
如有任何其它問題,請隨時與我聯絡。

湯尼 楊 敬啟

追蹤報價
Follow up Quotation

國貿關鍵字 ｜ 目標價格 ｜

目標價格 (target price)，買方對單一產品會依相關成本，估算出一個可接受的價格，對買方而言是越低越好，但對賣方同樣需維持一定的利潤，因此雙方對價格無法達成共識的情形下，賣方可要求買方提供其目標價格作為重新估算的參考。

情境說明

The seller follows up with the buyer regarding their comment on their 's quote.

賣方公司詢問買方公司對其報價單的意見。

角色介紹

買方｜Buyer: B, ABC Co., Ltd.

賣方｜Seller: S, Best International Trade Corp.

情境對話

S: We are wondering if you still want to go ahead with the order we talked about last week.

S：我想知道您是否能確定我們上週所談的那筆訂單？

B: Actually, it is the case. Our team have second thoughts about your product material, which we are inexperienced in.

B：事實上，是這樣的，我們的團隊對於您的產品材質有不同的想法，我們並不熟悉此材質。

S: The material of our product is different than other suppliers, but according to our annual sale report, the products sell well in the States and have a good market internationally. You can rest assured about the quality of our products.

S：我們產品的品質與其他供應商較不同，但根據我司的銷售報表，我們的產品在美國地區銷售很好，在國際市場亦是如此，您可以放心我們產品的品質。

B: Well. Another concern is its unit price is higher than our original suppliers.

B：好吧，我們另外的考量是貴司的產品單價高於我們原有供應商的價格。

S: Could you advise your target price for our reference?

S：可以告訴我貴司的目標價嗎？

B: The sales of this type dropped off during last quarter. The price adjustment will help to improve the sales. I'll do some calculation on the basis of current price and actual sales volume, and give you the figure.

B：這類產品的銷售量在上一季減少了，調整價格將有利於提高銷售量。
我會依現行價格和實際銷售量進行估算，再給你目標價。

S: That's fine. Let's return to the subject later on.

S：好的！我們回頭再來談論這件事。

情境說明

The buyer follows up with the seller regarding their comment on Best's quote.

賣方公司詢問買方公司對其報價單的意見。

角色介紹

買方｜Buyer: B, ABC Co., Ltd.

賣方｜Seller: S, Best International Trade Corp.

情境對話

S: I'm calling to confirm with you when we can expect your final decision on our official offer?

S：我打電話來是要跟您確認我們何時可以收到貴司對我們正式報價的最後決定。

B: We still need some time to think it over, but will ensure to reply you as soon as possible.

B：我們仍需要一些時間仔細考慮，但會確保儘速給您回覆。

S: Please be reminded that our offer remains open for 7 days. Please give me the answer by the day after tomorrow.

S：提醒您我司報價的有效期為7天，還請於後天前回覆我。

B: We'll have the department meeting to review suppliers' offer the day after tomorrow. Could you extend the offer period?

B：我們後天進行部門會議審閱供應商報價。您可以延長報價期限嗎？

S: I see. We will wait until next Monday.

S：瞭解，那我們會等到下週一。

B: Just a quick confirmation. Is the offer based on 20' container delivery, CIF delivery terms?

B：只是想簡單的確認一下，此報價是否依據20呎貨櫃及到岸價交貨條件。

S: Correct. Our offer is based on the trade terms as you required.

S：沒錯。我們的報價是依據您所要求的貿易條件。

關鍵字彙

⊘ **adjustment** *n.* [əˋdʒʌstmənt] 調整、調節

同義詞：regulation, accommodation

相關詞：adjustment inventory 調節庫存；adjustment process 調節過程

⊘ **improve** *v.* [ɪmˋpruv] 改善

同義詞：to make better, mend, meliorate

相關詞：improve facility 改善設備；improve service quality 改善服務品質

⊘ **figure** *n.* [ˋfɪgjɚ] 數字、金額、價格

同義詞：amount, number, digit

相關詞：figure of merit 質量指數；figure pattern 數字模式

⊘ **second thoughts** *ph.* 另外的想法

同義詞：additional thoughts, additional reflection

相關詞：think twice 重新考慮；thought spreading 思想傳播

⊘ **target price** *ph.* 目標價格

相關詞：ideal price 理想價格

drop off *ph.* 減少、衰落

同義詞：decrease, diminish, fall

相關詞：exports drop off 出口減少；drop off production 減產

definitely [ˈdɛfənɪtlɪ] *adv.* 肯定的、當然

同義詞：certainly, absolutely

相關詞：definitely offbeat 確實與眾不同

extend [ɪkˈstɛnd] *v.* 延長

同義詞：prolong, postpone

相關詞：extend the payment 付款延期；extend the deadline 延期

think over *ph.* 仔細考慮

同義詞：take into account

相關詞：think over and over 左思右想；think over the suggestion 仔細考慮這個建議

20′ container *ph.* 20呎貨櫃

相關詞：container port 貨櫃港

解　析：貨物出口分為散裝 (bulk) 及裝櫃 (container)，實務上常用的貨櫃尺寸有:

二十呎鋼製乾貨貨櫃 20′ Steel Dry Cargo Container

四十呎鋼製乾貨貨櫃 40′ Steel Dry Cargo Container

四十呎超高鋼製乾貨貨櫃 40′ Hi-Cube Steel Dry Cargo Container

四十呎超高冷凍櫃 40′ Hi-Cube Refrigerated Container

trade terms *ph.* 貿易條件

同義詞：terms of trade

相關詞：bilateral free trade 雙邊自由貿易

official offer *ph.* 正式報價

同義詞：formal offer, formal quotation

相關詞：offer for sale 公開發售

關鍵句型

be inexperienced in Sth.　不熟悉某事

例句說明：

· He **was inexperienced in** international trade.
他在國貿方面缺乏經驗。

· She **is** young and **inexperienced in** the world.
她年輕，不經世事。

on the basis of ...　根據

例句說明：

· The factory adjusted wages **on the basis of** increasing production.
工廠依據增加的生產量調整薪資。

· Tony selects the job **on the basis of** his qualifications.
湯尼依據其資歷選擇工作。

Please be reminded that ...　提醒您…

例句說明：

· **Please be reminded that** the due date of quotation is at the end of Mar.
提醒您一聲，報價到期日是在三月底。

remain open for ...　有效期為…

例句說明：

· The coupon **remains open for** one month.
該折價券有效期一個月。

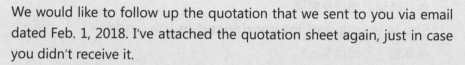

英文書信這樣寫

Follow up the Quotation 追蹤報價

Dear Tom,

We would like to follow up the quotation that we sent to you via email dated Feb. 1, 2018. I've attached the quotation sheet again, just in case you didn't receive it.

We are very eager to know if all the terms are acceptable and you'd like to proceed with the order. We hope that you could place the order at your earliest convenience and we can arrange to carry out the production for you immediately.

Our valve to be of high quality and with high functionality and were sure they will meet your requirements.

We are anxious to receive your order.

Sincerely yours,
Tony Yang

— 中文翻譯 —

湯姆 您好：

我們想要問問您關於我們在 2018 年 2 月 1 日 email 給您報價的事。我再附上報價單，以防您未收到。

我司很想知道貴司是否可以接受所有條件和需要下單。如果這些條件都可接受，希望您儘早下訂單，我們將立即排產。

深信我司具備高品質及高性能的特性，保證能符合您的需求。

期待收到貴司的訂單。

湯尼 楊 敬啟

職場經驗談

國際貿易出貨方式分為兩大類，整櫃貨及併櫃貨，整櫃貨指「同一」出口商的產品裝載於同一貨櫃並運送至同一交貨地；而併櫃貨是將「不同」出口商產品裝載於同一貨櫃運送至同一目的港後，再發貨到各個不同的收件地址。而併櫃貨運費計算方式則分為以重量噸計價或體積噸計價，計算公式如下：

貨物體積重之換算：
重量噸：1 Ton（噸）=1,000kgs
體積噸：1 M^3 =1CBM=1立方米

計算方法：
1 M=100 cm
1 M^3=100 cm X 100 cm X 100 cm
1 M^3=1 Cubic Meter =1 CBM

1材=1 Cubic Feet （英制）=1 $Feet^3$簡寫為1′
　　=1 feet X 1 fee X 1 feet（英呎）^{3}
　　=12" X 12" X 12" =1728 吋^3
　　=30.48 cm X 30.48 cm X 30.48 cm
　　=$(0.3048M)^3$
　　=0.02831684659M^3

∴1M^3=35.3146667239才（35.315）

（簡單的計算方式）
材數：每一外箱的長（CM）X 寬（CM）X 高（CM）÷28317（公式）=
材數 X 箱數÷35.315 = CBM（M^3）

議價成功或失敗
Success or Failure of Counter Offer

國貿關鍵字 ｜議價｜

議價在商場是很常見的，採購和業務人員的職責就是貨比三家，即使這個價錢是可以接受的，他們還是會試著殺一些，測試對方的底線，如果能找出因應之道對國貿人員的專業度是加分的。

情境說明

The buyer negotiates price with the seller and the seller accepts the counter-offer.

買方公司與賣方公司議價，賣方接受其所出的價格。

角色介紹

買方｜Buyer: B, ABC Co., Ltd.

賣方｜Seller: S, Best International Trade Corp.

情境對話

S: What did you think of our offer?

S：您對我們的報價有什麼想法？

B: I'm afraid that your price is higher than we can accept. Can you come down a little?

B：恐怕貴司的價格超出了我們所能接受的範圍，能稍微降價一些嗎？

S: We usually don't grant discount for small quantities.

B: How about if we order the same quantity every quarter? If the product is satisfactory, we will place repeated order with you.

S: Hmm, I can offer a 5% discount our list price.

B: It still overbalances our budget.

S: OK. Our maximum is 7%. But if you buy 500 units in the second year, I'll give you 10% discount. Only for VIP, we allow a rate of 10 % discount.

B: That might work, but we still need to give an internal discussion.

S: I hope you will accept our offer and give an order soon.

B: I see. I'll give you feedback within 24 hours.

S：對於小額訂單我們通常不給予折扣。

B：如果我們每季都向貴司下同樣數量的訂單呢？若是產品令我司滿意的話，我們將會下大量訂單給貴司。

S：那麼，我可以提供5％折扣。

B：這仍然超出我們的預算。

S：好吧！我方最大的折扣為7％，但如果貴司在第二年訂購500件，我們可提供給您10％的折扣。只有對重要客戶，我們才會給予10%的折扣。

B：這應該可行，但我們仍需要內部討論。

S：希望貴司能接受報價並儘快下訂單。

B：瞭解。我會在24小時內回覆您。

情境說明

The buyer negotiates price with the seller , and the seller rejects the counter-offer.

ABC公司與倍斯特公司議價，賣方倍斯特不接受其所出的價格。

角色介紹

買方│Buyer: B, ABC Co., Ltd.

賣方│Seller: S, Best International Trade Corp.

情境對話

B: Your offer is <u>too much higher than we anticipated</u>.

B：貴司的報價比我們預期的還高出許多。

S: The price is our minimum based on your order quantity.

S：依據貴司的訂購量，這已是我們的最低價了。

B: Is it possible for you to give us a lower price if we enlarge order size?

B：如果我們增加訂購量，是否能提供更低的價格？

S: If you can order 1000pcs more, then We can give you 5% special discount.

S：如果您的訂購量可以再多1000pcs，我們可以提供5%的優惠折扣。

B: Please consider another 5% discount, and that will be a workable deal for us.

B：如果可以再折5%，那對我們就是一筆可行的交易。

(After several day, the seller receive the buyer's call again.)

幾天後，買方接到賣方的來電

S: I'm sorry that your counter offer is unacceptable. We think our price is reasonable considering their high quality.

S：很抱歉我司無法接受貴司的還價，基於產品的高品質，我司認為我們的價格很合理。

B: We are satisfied with the quality and functionality of your product, but I don't find your price competitive.

B：我們非常滿意貴司的產品品質及性能，但此報價沒有競爭力。

S: Considering the cost of production, please understand it's our base price.

S：基於生產成本考量，請理解這已是我司的底價了。

B: If this is the case, it's highly regrettable that we have to decline your offer.

B：如果是這樣，非常遺憾我們不得不回絕貴司的報價。

關鍵字彙

⊘ **accept** *v.* 接受

同義詞：adopt, agree, consent to

相關詞：accept responsibility 承擔責任；inspect and then accept 驗收

⊘ **batch** *n.* [bætʃ] 批量

同義詞：lot, bundle

相關詞：batch number 批號；batch production 批量生產

⊘ **overbalance** *v.* [ˌovɚˈbæləns] 超額、超量

同義詞：outbalance, outweigh, to be off balance

相關詞：overbalance the disadvantages 利大於弊；weight overbalance 超重

⊘ **maximum** *a.* [`mæksəməm] 最高、至多

同義詞：the most, largest, biggest

相關詞：maximum demand 最大需求；maximum price 最高價

⊘ **come down** *ph.* 下來、沒落

同義詞：descend, fall, go down

相關詞：production costs come down 生產成本下降

⊘ **internal discussion** *ph.* 內部討論

同義詞：internal deliberation, discussion among ourselves

相關詞：department meeting 部門會議；conference call 電話會議

⊘ **acceptable** [ək`sɛptəb!] *a.* 可以接受的

同義詞：worthy of acceptance, satisfactory, desirable

相關詞：acceptable product 合格產品；acceptable risk 可接受的風險

⊘ **reasonable** *a.* [`riznəb!] 合理的

同義詞：sensible, rational

相關詞：fair and reasonable, just and reasonable 合情合理

⊘ **decline** *v.* [dɪ`klaɪn] 拒絕

同義詞：refuse, reject

相關詞：decline stage 衰退階段；decline period 衰退期

⊘ **counter offer** *ph.* 反報價、還價

相關詞：special offer 特價；official offer 正式報價

解　析：是指對報價者所提出之報價條件有一部分不能接受，但仍有交易意願，因此向賣方
提出新報價條件。反報價視為新要約，因此反報價提出後，將使原報價自動失效。

1 開發業務和價格條件

2

3

4

關鍵句型

I'm afraid that ... 我恐怕 …

例句說明：

· **I'm afraid** that the manager would reject your proposal.
恐怕經理會拒絕你的提案。

· **I'm afraid that** our factory is facing overcapacity situation.
恐怕我們工廠會面臨產能過剩的窘境。

give Sb. feedback 回覆某人

例句說明：

· I will reconsider your proposal and **give you feedback**.
我會再次考慮後回覆你。

· Can you **give me some feedback**?
可以給我一些回應嗎？

Sth. be too much ... than we expected. 比預期的更…

例句說明：

· The issue **is too much** more difficult **than we expected**.
該議題比我們所預期的更加棘手。

Sb. be satisfied with Sth. 某人對某事感到滿意

例句說明：

· **I am quite satisfied with** the shipment.
我們對這批貨相當滿意。

Counter Offer 還價

Dear Tony,

We appreciate your quotation offered to us on Feb. 1, 2018. Unfortunately, your price is too high for us to consider because it will leave us no margin of profit on our sales.

In consideration of the fact that we have done business with each other for many years and the number of our orders is increasing every year. Please consider offering 3% discount, and that will be an acceptable deal for us.

We sincerely hope you can accept our request and confirm by return soon.

Sincerely yours,
Tom Smith

– 中文翻譯 –

湯尼 您好：

感謝您2018年2月1日提供的報價。

很可惜，貴司的價格太高，超出我們所能考慮的範圍，如果以此價格購買產品，我們的銷售將無利潤。

有鑒於雙方生意往來多年，且我司的訂單量逐年成長。請考慮給予我司3%的折扣，對我們才會是一筆可行的交易。

真誠的希望貴司能接受我們的要求，並儘速回覆確認。

湯姆 史密斯 敬啟

Feedback to Counter Offer 回覆還價

Dear Tom,

We appreciate you let us know your counter offer by email, but we are sorry that we can't grant the discount due to the small quantity. We'd be willing to offer 2% special discount based on the MOQ 5000pcs. If you take our quality into consideration, we believe our price is favorable.

We hope you will reconsider and accept our offer.

Sincerely yours,
Tony Yang

― 中文翻譯 ―

湯姆 您好：

感謝貴司來信告知您的還價，然而很抱歉因為訂單量小，我司無法提供折扣。但在能符合最小訂購量5000件的基礎下，我們可以提供2%的特別折扣。若您考量到產品品質，我們的價格是有利的。

期望貴司再次考慮，並接受我司的報價。

湯尼 楊 敬啟

接受報價與調整價格
Acceptance of Quotation and Price Adjustment

國貿關鍵字 | 接受報價 |

　　賣方向買方報價後，待買方同意以此價格購買後，會下正式採購單，賣方再回覆交期和查詢庫存數量能否馬上符合訂單數量，買賣雙方再商討付款條件和運輸方式等。

情境說明

Buyer confirms to accept seller's offer.
買方公司確認接受賣方公司報價。

角色介紹

買方 | Buyer: B, ABC Co., Ltd.

賣方 | Seller: S, Best International Trade Corp.

情境對話

B: We have decided to accept your firm offer after internal meeting.

B：經過內部討論後，我司決定接受貴司的報價。

S: Great to hear that. How many pieces are you considering?

S：聽到這個消息真是太好了！請問貴司考慮下多少數量？

B: We'd like to <u>start with an order based on</u> your MOQ. If the sales are in excellent condition, we'll enlarge the order size.

B：我們想先依貴司最低訂購需求開始，如果銷售狀況佳，我們會再增加訂購量。

S: Perfect! We ensure that you will not regret it.

S：太好了！我保證您不會後悔的。

B: When can we expect to receive the Product?

B：預計何時可以收到產品？

S: As all our stock has been exhausted, we need to kick off new production run. Its lead time is 30 days from the date you place the order.

S：因我們庫存已全數耗盡，需要重新投產，生產週期是從下單日起算30天。

B: OK, I'll email you the formal order. Please countersign and return one copy to us for filing.

B：好的，我會 email 正式訂單給您，請簽署後回傳副本後我司歸檔。

S: No problem.

S：沒問題。

情境說明

The seller notifies the buyer about the price increasing.

賣方公司通知買方公司價格調漲事宜。

角色介紹

買方｜Buyer: B, ABC Co., Ltd.

賣方｜Seller: S, Best International Trade Corp.

情境對話

S: I'm calling to inform you we will raise the prices of our products.

S：我打電話是要通知您我司將會調漲價格。

B: What does it cause the prices going up?

B：什麼原因導致價格調漲呢？

S: It's largely for rising labor costs. Besides, we are also facing the situation for lack of raw materials.

S：主要是因為人工費用調漲。我們也面臨原物料短缺的問題。

B: What's the raising rate?

B：調漲幅度為何？

S: We'll increase about 15% to 20 %.

S：我們將調漲15%到20%。

B: Wow! It's a big price rise.

B：哇！這是一個很大的調幅。

S: Well, the prices are set based on the current market situation.

S：嗯，價格是依據現在市場情勢進行調整。

B: When do the new prices come into effect?

B：新價何時生效呢？

S: The new prices will be implemented at the end of the month. You may grasp the chance to buy our products at the current prices by the due date.

S：新價會從本月底開始時實施；貴司可把握機會在到期日前以現有價格購買產品。

B: Definitely. I'll estimate based on the market demand over the same period of last year and get back to you.

B：這是一定的，我會依據去年同期的市場需求進行預估，再回覆您。

關鍵字彙

✅ **consider** *v.* [kən`sɪdɚ] 考慮

同義詞：think, ponder, study, contemplate

相關詞：consider over and over again 思前想後；consider and decide 裁決

✅ **enlarge** *v.* [kən`sɪdɚ] 擴大

同義詞：widen, expand, broaden

相關詞：enlarge the production capacity 擴大產能；enlarge the sales amount 增加銷售量

✅ **firm offer** *ph.* 確定報價

相關詞：conditional offer 有條件報價；free offer 未定期限報價

解　析：確定報價是指報價人表明報價有效期限，且此期限內所列報價條件確定不變且有效。

⊘ **kick off** *ph.* 啟動、開始

同義詞：start up, embark on, commence

相關詞：project kick-off meeting 專案啟動會議；kick-off date 起始日

⊘ **production run** *ph.* 生產

相關詞：pre-production run 試產；production schedule 生產計劃

⊘ **lead time** *ph.* 週期、準備期

同義詞：interval

相關詞：delivery lead time 交貨時間；lead time for PPAP submission PPAP提交期間

（PPAP = Production Part Approval Process，指量產前的樣品提交及認證過程。）

⊘ **implement** *v.* [`ɪmpləmənt] 履行；實施；執行

同義詞：carry out, put into practice, execute, run

相關詞：implement the management 實施管理；implement the authority 行使權力

⊘ **estimate** *v.* [`ɛstə‚met] 估計、預計

同義詞：predict, calculate, evaluate

相關詞：estimated delivery date 預計出貨日；estimated cost 預估費用

⊘ **labor cost** *ph.* 人工成工

同義詞：labor charge

相關詞：labor cost advantage 勞力成本優勢；labor hours 工時

⊘ **come into effect** *ph.* 生效

同義詞：come into force, take effect, become effective

相關詞：come into effect upon signature 簽名後生效

關鍵句型

Sb. have/has decided to ... 　某人已決定…

例句說明：

- CEO **has decided to** give the green signal to the project.
  執行長已決定啟動這項專案。
- They **have decided to** stop cooperation with each other.
  他們已決定停止雙方合作關係。

start with Sth. based on ... 　從…開始著手進行

例句說明：

- Let's **start with** our discussion **based on** the easiest question.
  讓我們從最簡單的問題開始討論。
- They **start with** their cooperation **based on** a sample order.
  他們從一筆樣品訂單開始合作關係。

What reason causes ...? 　是什原因造成…？

例句說明：

- **What reason causes** our proposal rejected?
  我們提案失敗的原因為何？

grasp the chance to ... 　把握機會…

例句說明：

- You should **grasp the chance to** get the business during this visit.
  你應該在這次拜訪時，把握機會得到訂單。

Notification of Price Adjustment 調價通知

Dear Customers,

It is with our greatest regret that we must announce that we are going to raise the prices of our products from March 1, 2018.

Because of the continual rise in the labor cost and higher production cost, we have been forced to raise the prices based on the market mechanism. The rise rate is up to 10% ~ 20%.

However, the prices are still on the low side compared with other competitors'. Please find the enclosed price list up to date for your reference.

Kindly be reminded that the new prices will become effective at the end of the month. From that day on, the new orders will be carried out based on the new prices accordingly.

Your kind understanding of our situation and continual support will be highly appreciated.

Sincerely yours,
Tony Yang

— 中文翻譯 —

親愛的客戶：

很遺憾通知您，我司將從2018年3月1日起調漲產品價格。

因持續調漲的工資及高生產成本，我司被迫不得不依據市場機制調漲價格，調漲比率達10%至20%。然而，跟其它競爭者價格相比，此價格是偏低。請參考附件最新報價單。

提醒您，新價格將從本月底開始生效。此後，新訂單會依據新價格處理。

希望（貴司）能理解我司立場，繼續給予支持，我們將不勝感激。

湯尼 楊 敬啟

知識補給

出口價格估算：

FOB售價 = FOB成本價＋FOB售價 x（銀行手續費率＋推廣費率＋押匯貼現率＋商港建設費率＋利潤率）

移項後得：

$$FOB售價 = \frac{FOB\ 成本價}{1-（銀行手續費率＋推廣費率＋押匯貼現率＋商港建設費率＋利潤率）}$$

CFR 售價＝CFR成本價＋CFR售價（手續費率＋貼現率＋利潤率）＋商港建設費＋推廣費

移項後得：

$$CFR\ 售價 = \frac{CFR\ 成本價＋商港建設費＋推廣費}{1-（手續費率＋貼現率＋利潤率）}$$

CIF售價＝CFR成本價＋CIF售價x1.1x保險費率＋（手續費率＋貼現率＋利潤率）**x CIF售價**＋商港建設費＋推廣費

移項後得：

$$CIF售價 = \frac{CFR成本價＋商港建設費＋推廣費}{1-（1.1\ x保險費率＋手續費率＋貼現率＋利潤率）}$$

簽署合約
Sign a Contract

國貿關鍵字 | 國貿契約 |

　　一般而言，貿易雙方在開始合作關係前會簽訂合約，訂定雙方未來合作方式，作為未來解決可能之糾紛或訴訟時之法律依據。首先針對口頭上商議的內容草擬成文字，即形成所謂的草約（draft contract），雙方就交易的條款達成一致意見後，就進入正式合約簽訂階段。在簽約前，可對對方進行信用調查，並要求簽約者提供相關法律檔，證明其合法資格，如為代為處理簽約事宜者，須要求提供正式書面授權證明，以確保合約的合法性和有效性。合約內容定義貿易雙方交易的基本條款（產品、品質、價格、包裝、保險、交貨及付款）及一般條款（檢驗、索賠、不可抗力、仲裁、適用法條及匯率變動等），條款內容務必明確、具體及一致，以避免未來執行過程中出現爭議。

情境說明

The seller negotiates the terms of draft contract with the buyer.

倍斯特公司與ABC公司協商草約條款。

角色介紹
買方 | Buyer: B, ABC Co., Ltd.
賣方 | Seller: S, Best International Trade Corp.

情境對話

B: Tony, I have sent you the draft contract according to our discussion. Do you have any question regarding the terms of the contract?

B：湯尼，我已將根據我們的討論所擬的草約寄給您。針對合約上的條款，您有任何問題嗎？

S: About the payment terms, I am wondering if you can work on 30 % in advance and balance pay-off in 30 days from bill of lading date.

S：關於付款條件，不知貴司可否接受30%預付餘款提單日起30天內付清的條件。

B: It's not our regular practice about the terms of payment.

B：這並非我司一般採用的付款方式。

S: We hope you could be more flexible on this condition.

S：我們希望貴司在這項條件上能更彈性些。

B: Hmmm... This is a great concession, but we can give it a try.

B：嗯⋯這是很大的讓步，但我們可以試試看。

S: Excellent Thanks!

S：好極了謝您！

B: Now we have settled the terms of payment. Any concern about other elements of the contract including delivery, shipment terms, insurance terms and so on?

B：現在我們已經談妥了付款條件。對合約上的其它要件，包括交貨期、裝運條款、保險條款等，您有任何意見嗎？

S: We have no objection with the other terms.

S：我們對其它條款沒有異議。

B: I'll revise the terms per our discussion just now and submit the revised contract for your review.

B：我會就方才討論的內容修改條款，再提供修改過的合約供您檢視。

情境說明

The seller confirms the terms of contract with the buyer.

倍斯特公司與ABC公司確認合約條款。

情境對話

B: Hi! Tony, I'm calling to enquire if you have a close study of the contract in duplicate we sent to you last Friday.

S: We have already looked through all the terms of the contract.

B: If you have no objection to the contract, we hope we can sign the contract with each other as soon as possible.

S: I have to say that we still think your payment terms are strict for us. We have given in to the conditions to show our sincerity to cooperate with you.

B: 湯尼 您好！我打來是要問您是否仔細閱讀上週五我們寄給您一式兩份合約。

S: 我們已經檢視合約上的所有條款。

B: 如貴司就合約內容無異議，希望我們可以盡速簽約，開始雙方合作關係。

S: 我必須說我司仍認為貴司的付款條件太嚴苛。我們讓步接受是為了顯示與貴司合作的誠意。

1 開發業務和價格條件 CHAPTER

2

3

4

B: We feel greatly beholden to you for your kindness and expect to develop mutually beneficial and win-win cooperation with you.

B：承蒙貴司厚愛，十分感激，並期待與貴司發展互利雙贏的合作關係。

S: It would be our pleasure.

S：這是我們的榮幸。

B: Would you please return us one copy of the contract, duly countersigned?

B：煩請會簽合約後寄回副本一份。

S: I'll sign the contract immediately to start our cooperation.

S：我會立即簽約來開始我們的合作關係。

B: I must thank you again for your generous support and do believe our cooperation will be a great success.

B：我要再次感謝貴司的慷慨支持，並深信我們的合作將會非常成功。

關鍵字彙

✓ **terms** *n.* [tɝm] 條件，條款
同義詞：condition, clause
相關詞：make terms, come to terms 達成協議

✓ **practice** *n.* [`præktɪs] 實行，實施
同義詞：exercise
相關詞：in practice 實際上；put into practice 實施

✓ **flexible** *a.* [`flɛksəb!] 順從的，可彎曲的
同義詞：pliable, pliant, yielding
相關詞：flexible benefits 靈活福利；flexible exchange rates 浮動匯率

⊘ **concession** *n.* [kənˋsɛʃən] 讓步

同義詞：conceding, yielding

相關詞：mutual concession 雙方讓步；make concession 做出讓步

⊘ **objection** *n.* [əbˋdʒɛkʃən] 反對，異議

同義詞：dissent, disapproval, opposition

相關詞：to raise an objection 提出異議

⊘ **revise** *v.* [rɪˋvaɪz] 修改

同義詞：amend, edit

相關詞：revise and enlarge 增訂；revised edition 修訂版

⊘ **enquire** *v.* [ɪnˋkwaɪr] 詢問

同義詞：ask, inquire

相關詞：enquire about train 查詢火車班次

⊘ **duplicate** *n.* [ˋdjupləkɪt] 副本

同義詞：transcript

相關詞：in duplicate 一式兩份；duplicate bill of lading 副本提單

⊘ **beholden** *a.* [bɪˋholdən] 蒙恩的

同義詞：indebted, obligated

相關詞：greatly beholden 十分感激

⊘ **given in** to *ph.* 讓步

同義詞：give way to, yield to, submit to

相關詞：give in to difficulties 向困難屈服

⊘ **mutually** beneficial *ph.* 雙方互利

同義詞：interdependent

相關詞：mutually beneficial relationships 雙方互利關係

✓ win-win *ph.* 雙贏
同義詞：profitable to both sides
相關詞：win-win situation 雙贏局面

關鍵句型

It's not our regular practice about Sth. 這並非我們對某事的習慣方式

例句說明：

· **It's not our regular practice about** cooperation with foreign customers.
這並非我們一般與國外客戶合作的模式。

be more flexible on Sth. 在某事上更彈性

例句說明：

· It will be appreciated if you could **be more flexible on** MOQ.
若貴司在最小訂購量上能更放寬些，我司將不勝感激。

I have to say ... 我必須說…

例句說明：

· **I have to say** another regulation.
我必須說一下另一項規定。

Sb. feel greatly beholden ... 某人十分感激…

例句說明：

· **She feel greatly beholden** to you for your help.
她對於你的協助十分感激。

Submit Draft Contract 提出草約

Dear Tony,

According to our discussion, attached please find our draft contract in duplicate for your reference.

Please check the terms of the draft, and keep us informed if you have any concern. We can have a conference call to further discuss the subject if needed.

We await your prompt reply.

Sincerely yours,
Tom Smith

– 中文翻譯 –

湯尼 您好：

依據我們討論的內容，請參閱附件草約副本。

請檢視草約中的條款，並告知貴司對草約內容是否有其它顧慮。如果有需要，我們可以進行電話會議進一步討論此議題。.

期待您的盡速回覆。

湯姆 史密斯 敬啟

Discussion of Draft Contract 草約討論

Dear Tom,

We'd like to inform you that we have different thoughts regarding some terms of the draft contract, especially the payment terms.

I think we might require a renegotiation of the terms and would suggest to have a video conference at 10 o'clock on Monday morning if it is convenient for you. Or else, please advise your available time.

Please give us your reply as soon as possible.

Sincerely yours,
Tony Yang

— 中文翻譯 —

湯姆 您好：

藉由此信通知貴司我們對於草約上的某些條款有不同看法，尤其針對付款條件。

我想我們需要就條款內容重新協商。如果您方便，我司建議下週一早上十點進行視訊會議。或者，請告知您方便的時間。

請協助盡快回覆。

湯尼 楊 敬啟

下採購訂單
Place Purchase Order

國貿關鍵字 | 下訂單流程 |

> 買方下正式訂單給賣方後，賣方確認庫存量和生產量可符合訂單，就回簽訂單和回覆交期，如果買方也回覆同意交期，這張訂單即算成立。

情境說明

The buyer places an order to the seller. .
買方公司下緊急訂單給賣方公司。

角色介紹

買方 | Buyer: B, ABC Co., Ltd.

賣方 | Seller: S, Best International Trade Corp.

情境對話

B: Hello, Tony. I'm calling you about placing PO for the new balance valve.

B：您好！湯尼。我打來是要下單訂購新平衡閥。

S: No problem! Just send the PO as usual and we will confirm the delivery date by return.

S：沒問題！你就跟先前一樣下訂單給我們，我司會回覆確認交期。

B: The problem is that we need this lot urgently, as our stock is nearly exhausted. We will appreciate if you can make the shipment without delay.

S: As you know, we normally keep stock levels low.

B: That's why I'm calling you personally to check this issue.

S: How many pieces and which size do you require?

B: We need 100 pieces each of 3/4" and 1/2". How soon can you dispatch the order?

S: I can arrange immediate shipment if we have that quantity available.

B: Great. I'll send the formal PO after the call. Please countersign with your earliest delivery date and send by return.

S: I will.

B： 問題是我們急需要此批貨，因為我們的庫存快要消耗完了。如貴司能立即安排出貨，我們將不勝感激。

S： 您知道，我們通常庫存不多。

B： 這就是我親自打來問這事的原因。

S： 您需要多少數量及哪一個尺寸？

B： 我們需要3/4 英吋及1/2英吋各100件。您多快可以安排出貨？

S： 如果我們有這些量，我可以立即安排出貨。

B： 太好了。通完話後我會下正式訂單，請回簽並提供最快交期。

S： 我會的。

The seller confirms receipt of order from the buyer..

賣方公司確定接收買方公司下的緊急訂單。

情境對話

S: Hi, Tom. I'm calling to confirm on the receipt of your PO number 1234.

S：湯姆。您好！我打電話來是要跟您確認收到貴司單號為1234的訂單。

B: Thanks When can I expect to receive the order?

B：謝謝。我們何時可以收到貨物呢？

S: Unfortunately, our certain stock is insufficient to fulfill your demand, but we can kick off an urgent production run.

S：抱歉，目前的庫存不夠供應您所需的數量，但我們可以立即開始緊急生產。

B: How soon can the products be ready for delivery?

B：多快可以準備完成出貨？

S: I can make sure the production will be finished within two weeks.

S：我可以保證在兩周內完成生產。

B: In this case, we <u>won't be able to</u> catch the season <u>if</u> the order is sent by sea. Then we may be forced to choose air freight for receiving the goods quicker.

B：如果是這樣，以海運出貨將無法趕上我們的銷售季。那我們就得要選擇空運，才能快點收到產品。

S: I'm afraid so.

S：恐怕是如此。

B: OK, Let's do it that way. Just ensure to make the punctual shipment.

B：好吧！就這麼做吧！只要確認能準時出貨即可。

S: Certainly. I'll send back the purchase confirmation.

S：這是當然的，我會寄回購貨確認書。

關鍵字彙

✓ **lot** *n.* [lɑt] 一批貨
同義詞：batch
相關詞：lot production 成批生產

✓ **exhaust** *v.* [ɪgˋzɔstɪd] 耗盡
同義詞：use up, consume
相關詞：exhausted battery 用完的電池

✓ **require** *v.* [rɪˋkwaɪr] 需要
同義詞：need, want, demand
相關詞：required course 必修課

⊘ **dispatch** *v.* [dɪˋspætʃ] 發送

同義詞：send off, carry, deliver

相關詞：dispatch boat 通信船；dispatch date 出貨日

⊘ **immediate** *a.* [ɪˋmidɪɪt] 立即

同義詞：at once, forthwith

相關詞：immediate impact 直接影響；immediate feedback 及時反饋

⊘ **delivery date** *ph.* 出貨日

同義詞：dispatch date, release date

相關詞：closing date 結關日；on board date 裝船日；latest shipment date 最後裝船日

⊘ **insufficient** *a.* [ˌɪnsəˋfɪʃnt] 不充足的

同義詞：not enough, inadequate, lacking

相關詞：insufficient funds 資金不足；insufficient evidence 證據不足

⊘ **fulfill** *v.* [fʊlˋfɪl] 滿足

同義詞：satisfy, supply

相關詞：self-fulfilling 自我實現的；fulfill the promise 履行承諾

⊘ **in this case** *ph.* 既然如此

同義詞：in this situation, if so

相關詞：case by case 視個別狀況；case in point 這方面的例證

⊘ **punctual** *a.* [ˋpʌŋktʃʊəl] 準時的

同義詞：on schedule, on time

相關詞：punctual arrival 準時抵達；punctual person 守時的人

⊘ **catch the season** *ph.* 趕上銷售季

同義詞：catch the sales season

相關詞：peak season, peak period, busy season 旺季；slack season, dull season, off season 淡季

✅ **purchase confirmation** *ph.* 購貨確認書

相關詞：SC（sales confirmation） 銷貨確認書；SC（sales contract）銷售合約；
purchase contract 購貨合約

解　析：合約多用於大宗商品或金額大的交易，合約內容全面且詳細。確認書則適用於成交
金額不大、批數較多的產品。合約及確認書兩者皆具同等法律效力。

關鍵句型

I can arrange ... if .... 　如果⋯，我可以安排⋯

例句說明：

· **I can arrange** the transportation and accommodation **if** you plan to attend the trade show.
如果你計畫參展，我可以安排交通及住宿事宜。

Sb. be not able to ..., if ... 　如果⋯，某人就無法⋯

例句說明：

· We **aren't be able to** smooth the tight production capacity, **if** the problem of insufficient staff still exists.
如果缺工問題仍存在，我們就無法舒緩產能緊張狀況。

79

下採購單 Place Purchase Order

Dear Tony

We are satisfied with your May 23th offer Atlched please find our PO number 1234.

Please be informed that we are in urgent need of the goods. Your prompt attention to this order with earliest delivery will be greatly appreciated.
We hope to receive your prompt reply.

Sincerely yours,
Tom Smith

— 中文翻譯 —

湯尼 您好：

我司非常滿意貴司於5月23日提供的報價。在此附上我司單號1234的訂單。

在此通知您我們急需此批貨，如果您能儘速處理此訂單並儘早出貨，我司將不勝感激。

希望儘快收到您的回覆。

湯姆 史密斯 敬啟

確認訂單 Order Confirmation

Dear Tom,

We are delighted to receive your PO number 1234 with many thanks.

We can dispatch the goods immediately per your requirement. Attached is the purchase confirmation for your file. We'll notify the estimated delivery date as soon as receiving your advance payment.

Please feel free to contact us for any further requirement.

Sincerely yours,
Tony Yang

─ 中文翻譯 ─

湯姆 您好:

很高興收到貴司單號 1234 的訂單，謝謝。

我們可以依據貴司的要求立即安排出貨。附件是購貨確認書供您留存，待收到貴司預付款後，我們會告知預計出貨日。

如您有任何其他要求，請隨時與我們聯絡任何進一步要求。

湯尼 楊 敬啟

更改和取消訂單
Order Change and Order Cancellation

國貿關鍵字 | 訂單變動 |

客戶對已經開始生產的訂單進行追加或減量是很常見的情況,但賣方需要注意是否能夠維持同一個交期,因為買方會希望節省運費或是即時趕上工廠生產線,而要求合併出貨。賣方可能需要以追加訂單的時間來判斷是否可以給同一個交期,跟客戶溝通如何不壓縮自己的交貨時間,也能滿足客戶的需求。

情境說明

The buyer requests to change the quantity on the order placed to the seller.

買方公司要求更改已下給賣方公司的訂單數量。

角色介紹

買方 | Buyer: B, ABC Co., Ltd.

賣方 | Seller: S, Best International Trade Corp.

情境對話

B: Hi, Tony. I want to change an active order with you.

S: Yes, Tom. Please give me the reference number on the proforma invoice to locate your order details from ERP system.

B:湯尼。您好!我想要更改一張現有的訂單。

S:好的,湯姆。請給我形式發票上的參考號碼,讓我從ERP系統來查您的訂單詳細資訊。

B: The reference number is 4321.

B：參考號碼是 4321。

S: Let me see. Your order quantity is 100 pieces each of 3/4″ and 1/2″ balance valve.

S：讓我看看，您訂單數量是 3/4″ 和 1/2″ 的平衡閥各100件。

B: Exactly. We need to increase the order quantity to 150 pieces per each size. <u>Is it still time to</u> catch the current production?

B：沒錯，我們需要增加訂單數量，每個尺寸各150件。請問是否仍趕得上一起生產？

S: Sorry that we cannot accept your quantity increase because the certain production is now in progress.

S：很抱歉，我們不能接受您增加數量，因為現正已經開始生產了。

B: <u>May we request your special favor</u> by arranging the further space for our additional demand?

B：可否請您特別幫忙，針對我司額外需求排進生產？

S: Please kindly understand that it's really difficult for new material preparation with the increased small quantity.

B：還請您諒解要為小額增量，準備新材量是很有困難的。

情境說明

The buyer requests to cancel the quantity on the order placed to the seller.

買方公司要求取消已下給賣方公司的訂單數量。

情境對話

B: Hi, Tony. I'm glad I managed to catch you.

B：您好，湯尼。很高興終於聯絡上你。

S: Hello, Tom. <u>Is there anything particular</u> you want to discuss?

S：你好，湯姆。有什麼特別要跟我討論的事情嗎？

B: I'm sorry that we have to cancel the PO number 5678.

B：很抱歉我們不得不取消單號為5678 的訂單。

S: Any reason of the sudden change?

S：突然有這樣的變化是什麼原因呢？

B: Our new sales figure shows the new type of the ball valve hasn't sold as well as anticipated.

B：我們新的銷售數字顯示這款新型球閥的銷售不如預期。

S: I regret to hear that. Please understand that we cannot accept your order cancellation because we have purchased all raw materials.

S：很遺憾聽到這個消息。請諒解我們不能接受取消訂單，因為我們所有的原料都已購入了。

B: <u>Is there any chance to</u> make a partial reduction?

S: I'm afraid that we can't agree as this is customized special specifications for your company, the non-standard products.

B：有沒有可能作部分減量呢？

S：恐怕我們無法這樣做，因為這是為貴司客製化的特殊規格品。

關鍵字彙

⊘ **active** *a.* [ˋæktɪv] 活潑的、在進展中的、現行的
同義詞：vivacious, lively
相關詞：active account 有效帳戶

⊘ **locate** *v.* [loˋket] 找出
同義詞：find, search out, discover
相關詞：locating 定位

⊘ **additional** *a.* [əˋdɪʃən!] 額外的
同義詞：supplementary, extra
相關詞：additional article 增訂條款；additional cargo 加載貨

⊘ **preparation** *n.* [͵prɛpəˋreʃən] 準備
同義詞：provision, arrangement
相關詞：preparation work 準備工作；preparation room 準備室

⊘ **ERP system** *ph.* 企業資源計劃系統
解　析：ERP（Enterprise Resource Planning），由美國著名管理諮詢公司Gartner Group Inc. 於1990年提出，ERP 系統能將企業內部所有資源整合在一起，對採購、生產、成本、庫存、銷售、運輸、財務、人力資源進行規畫，以達到資源優化配置。

⊘ **in progress** *ph.* 進行中

同義詞：progressing, in the middle of

相關詞：work in progress 進展中的工作；recording in progress 錄音中

⊘ **particular** *a.* [pəˈtɪkjələ] 特殊的

同義詞：special, unusual, especially

相關詞：particular thanks 特別感謝；go into particulars 詳細敘述

⊘ **cancellation** *n.* [ˌkæns!ˈeʃən] 取消

同義詞：revocation, nullification

相關詞：cancellation of business license 吊銷執照；cancellation of representation 解除代理

⊘ **partial** *a.* [ˈpɑrʃəl] 部分

同義詞：fractional, fragmentary

相關詞：partial assembly 部件裝配；partial to 偏袒

⊘ **reduction** *n.* [rɪˈdʌkʃən] 減少

同義詞：decreas, loss, lessening

相關詞：a reduction in production 減產；price reduction 降價

⊘ **customized** *a.* [ˈkʌstəmˌaɪz] 客製化的

同義詞：specialized, custom-built, personalized

解　析：客製化指依據各客戶不同需求，製造並提供符合單一客戶需求的產品，反之則為標準化（standardization）。

1
開發業務和價格條件

2

3

4

關鍵句型

Is it still time to ... ? 是否仍有足夠的時間…

例句說明：

· **Is it still time to** arrange the production plan of this month?
是否仍有足夠的時間排上本月的生產排程？

May we request your special favor ... 我們能否要求你特別幫忙 …

例句說明：

· **May we request your special favor** to accelerate the production progress for our open orders?
我們能否要求你特別幫忙，加快我們現有訂單的生產進度？

Is there anything particular (that) ... 有什麼特殊的事…？

例句說明：

· Is there anything particular that you want to raise up in the production & promotion meeting?
有什麼特殊的事項你想要在產銷會議中提出來討論嗎？

Is there any chance to ... 是否有機會…？

例句說明：

· Is there any chance to accelerate the production progress?
請問有可能加速生產進度嗎？

英文書信這樣寫

更改訂單 Order Change

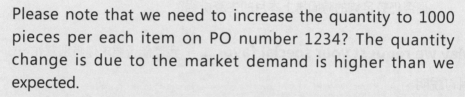

Dear Tony,

Please note that we need to increase the quantity to 1000 pieces per each item on PO number 1234? The quantity change is due to the market demand is higher than we expected.

We'll send the revised order later. Please confirm if the delivery date can be remained without change by return. Besides, due to the larger order size, I'd like to know inquire to see if there is any room for a downward regulation of piece price.

Please favor us with your reply as early as possible.

Yours sincerely,
Tom Smith

- 中文翻譯 -

湯尼 您好：

請求貴司注意我們需要將單號1234的訂單其每個品項增加數量到1000件，所以更改數量是因為市場需求高於我們預期。

我們會稍後會發給您修改後的訂單。請您回覆確認交期是否不變。此外由於訂單數量較大，我也想詢問看是否產品單價有調降的空間。

請協助儘速回覆。

湯姆 史密斯 敬啟

取消訂單 Order Cancellation

Dear Tony,

Much to my regret, we have to cancel our PO number 5678. We just found that we overstocked on some items due to our system error.

Please advise if you could accept the order cancellation. Or else, please grant us a big favor to accept a partial reduction as following:

P/N 00008 to be reduced from 100pcs to 50pcs
P/N 00009 to be reduced from 150pcs to 50pcs

We apologize again for any inconvenience it may have caused, and look forward to your reply.

Yours sincerely,
Tom Smith

－ 中文翻譯 －

湯尼 您好：

很遺憾，我司必須取消單號為5678的訂單，由於系統錯誤，我們剛剛發現有些品項的庫存過剩。

請告知是否可接受取消訂單。或者，能否幫忙接受如下的減量提議：

P/N 00008 從100pcs 減少至 50pcs
P/N 00009 從150pcs 減少至 50pcs

很抱歉造成貴司任何的困擾，期待您的回音。

湯姆 史密斯 敬啟

訂單未成立
Order Rejection or Follow-up Order

　　適逢客戶大量下單的生產旺季，買方可先主動聯絡客戶詢問是否下單和對方下單時間，除了能多接訂單，也可以預先安排產能。同時也提醒客人盡早下訂單，賣方也有較充裕的生產和運輸時間，滿足買方對貨物和交期要求。

情境說明

The buyer rejects the new order placed by the seller due to the fault in facility.

因生產設備故障，賣方公司無法接受買方公司的新訂單。

角色介紹

買方 | Buyer: B, ABC Co., Ltd.

賣方 | Seller: S, Best International Trade Corp.

情境對話

S: We received your PO number 1122 yesterday. Do your company required 2000 pieces of ball valve.

B: It's correct. Something wrong with that?

S：我們昨天收到貴司單號為1122的訂單。貴司需求2000件球閥是嗎？

B：沒錯，有什麼不對勁的嗎？

S: We are unable to fulfill your order as our forging machine has broken down and must be replaced.

S：我們沒辦法完成您的訂單，因我們的鍛造機損壞了，必須進行更換。

B: Oh, that's terrible. How soon can you solve the problem?

B：噢，那太糟糕了。您多快能解決這問題呢？

S: To make matters worse, the manufacturer isn't really sure when the repair work will be completed owing to the shortage of spare parts.

S：更糟的是，因為零件短缺，製造商也無法確定何時可完成維修工作。

B: In this case, we will have to control our stock levels to avoid shortage.

B：在這種情況下，我們必須控制庫存水準，以避免產品短缺。

S: We will contact you immediately once the production is restored. Really sorry for any inconvenience caused to you.

S：一旦恢復生產，我們會立即與您聯繫。真的很抱歉造成您的任何不便。

B: That's all right.

B：沒關係。

情境說明

The seller presses an old customer to place a new order.

賣方公司向老客戶跟催訂單。

角色介紹

買方 | Buyer: B, ABC Co., Ltd.

賣方 | Seller: S, Best International Trade Corp.

情境對話

S: Hi, Monica. This is Tony Yang from Best Corp.

B: Hello, Tony. Nice to hear from you. How have you been lately, my lad?

S: Not so bad. Well, we have not received your order since last June. Is the negligence of our service caused you to discontinue our cooperation?

B: Believe it or not, I'm just going to call you to talk about a new order.

S: Great to hear that. As you know, it's on season and our production is in high gear. We would advise you to place order without loss of time.

S：您好,莫妮卡,我是倍斯特公司的湯尼 楊。

B：你好,湯尼,很高興聽到你的消息。最近如何,老弟?

S：不錯。是這樣的,從去年6月起我們就沒收到貴司的訂單,是我們服務不周使得您不再與我們合作嗎?

B：相信嗎,我正要打電話給您談一筆新訂單。

S：很高興聽到這個消息。正如你所知,現在正是旺季,而我們的生產正積極進行中,還請您把握時間,趕緊下訂單。

B: Thank you for the reminder. The order sheet is under final review and should be sent to you tomorrow.

B: Perfect. Iam really glad to talk to you today. Please never hesitate to share your suggestion or comments with us so that we can provide you a better service.

S: I will.

B：謝謝您的提醒。我們的訂單在最後審查中，明天應可發送給您。

B：好極了。今天真的很高興能與您聊聊。請儘管與我們分享您的建議或意見，以便讓我們為您提供更好的服務。

S：我會的。

關鍵字彙

○ **replace** *v.* [rɪ`ples] 代替，更換

同義詞：change, renew

相關詞：remove and replace 取而代之；replaceability 可替換性

○ **terrible** *a.* [`tɛrəb!] 糟糕的

同義詞：awful, deplorable, too bad

相關詞：terrible mess 凌亂不堪；terrible news 可怕的消息

○ **solve** *v.* [sɑlv] 解決

同義詞：resolve, settle, work out

相關詞：problem-solving 解決問題；be unable to solve 無解

○ **repair work** *ph.* 維修工作

同義詞：maintenance work

相關詞：repair expenses 修理費；repair cycle 檢修週期

⊘ **owing to** *ph.* 由於

同義詞：because of, by reason of, by virtue of

相關詞：owing to lack of experience 由於缺乏經驗

⊘ **shortage** *n.* [ˋʃɔrtɪdʒ] 不足

同義詞：lack, deficiency, scarcity

相關詞：labor shortage 勞工短缺；shortage of funds 資金短缺

⊘ **restore** *v.* [rɪˋstor] 恢復

同義詞：recover, regain, resume

相關詞：restore the function 恢復功能；restore order 恢復秩序

⊘ **negligence** *n.* [ˋnɛglɪdʒəns] 疏忽

同義詞：omission, oversight, disregard

相關詞：negligence of duty 玩忽職守；gross negligence 重大疏失

⊘ **discontinue** *v.* [ˌdɪskənˋtɪnju] 停止，中斷

同義詞：break off, stop, suspend

相關詞：discontinue the agreement 解除合約；discontinue use 停止使用

⊘ **stage** *n.* [stedʒ] 階段

同義詞：section, period

相關詞：initial stage 初期；late stage 後期；early stage 早期

⊘ **on season** *ph.* 正處旺季

相關詞：tourist season 旅遊旺季；shopping season 購物旺季

⊘ **in high gear** *ph.* 積極進行

同義詞：put into practice actively

相關詞：actively participate 積極參與

關鍵句型

We are unable to ... 我們無法…

例句說明：

· **We are unable to** meet the due date.

我們無法符合到期日要求。

· **We are unable to** accept the target price.

我們無法接受此目標價。

We will contact you immediately once ... 當… 時，我們會立即連絡你

例句說明：

· **We will contact you immediately once** facilities resume.

待設備恢復運作後，我們會立即聯絡你。

· **We will contact you immediately once** the shipment is ready for dispatch.

待產品備妥可出貨時，我們會立即聯絡你。

Is the negligence of ... caused you ... 是否因為…的疏失導致你…

例句說明：

· **Is the negligence of** operation **caused** the system to shut down?

是因為操作疏失導致系統當機嗎？

We would advise .... without ... 我們奉勸…不要…

例句說明：

· **We would advise** the QA to implement the inspection in detail **without** skipping any batch.

我們會勸告品保詳細檢驗，不要跳檢任一批次。

拒接訂單 Order Rejection

Dear Tom,

We are in receipt of your order number 3344 sent by email dated March 30. To our greatest regret we have to inform you that we cannot at present fulfill any new orders, due to the tight production capacity. We are, however, keeping your order before us. As soon as we are in a position to accept new orders, we will send you an email.

Let me reiterate our sincere regret. and your kind understanding will be appreciated.

Sincerely yours,
Tony Yang

― 中文翻譯 ―

湯姆 您好：

我司收到您3月30日寄出單號為3344的訂單，非常遺憾通知貴司，由於產能吃緊，我司需在此通知無法接受任何新訂單。然而，我們會保留貴司訂單，如果可以開始接單時，我司將立即 email 通知貴司。

請容我再次因此問題致上誠摯的歉意，若您能理解我司的立場，我們將不勝感激。

湯尼 楊 敬啟

1
開發業務和價格條件

2

3

4

催促訂單 Pressing for Follow-Up Order

Dear Monica,

We have not heard from you for a certain period. We hope everything is going well for all staff of your company.

As we have not received your order since last June, we're wondering if our service didn't satisfy you. It is our policy to render the best service to our customers, especially you, one of our most important business partners. Any suggestion or comments from you will be greatly welcomed and appreciated.

We look forward to receiving your further comments.

Sincerely yours,
Tony Yang

－ 中文翻譯 －

夢妮卡 您好：

已有一段時間沒有聽到貴司的消息。願貴司全體同仁一切安好。

由於從去年六月起就沒再收到貴司的訂單，不知是否我們的服務有令您不滿意的地方。我們公司的政策就是提供最好的服務予客戶，尤其貴司是我們最重要的生意夥伴之一。我司十分歡迎及感激貴司提供的任何建議或意見。

我們期待收到貴司的回信。

湯尼 楊 敬啟

付款條件和保險條件

Payment terms and insurance terms

信用狀付款條件
Payment Terms as L/C

國貿關鍵字 | 信用狀 |

信用狀(Letter of Credit, L/C) 是一種銀行開立的有條件並承諾付款的書面文件，即代表銀行的信用。信用狀是銀行(即開狀行)依照進口商(即開狀申請人)的要求和指示，對出口商(即受益人)發出的、授權出口商簽發以銀行或進口商為付款人的匯票，保證在提交符合信用狀條款規定的匯票和單據時，必定承兌和付款的保證文件。在國際貿易中主要是以跟單信用狀為主。

情境說明

The buyer accepts the payment terms of L/C by the seller .

買方公司同意賣方公司要求以信用狀為付款條件。

角色介紹
買方 | Buyer: B, ABC Co., Ltd.
賣方 | Seller: S, Best International Trade Corp.

情境對話

B: Hi, Tony. I want to discuss the payment terms against our P/O No. 1234.

B：您好，湯尼，我想要跟您討論我司訂單號碼1234的付款條件。

S: Is there a problem?

S：有什麼問題嗎？

B: Could you make an exception to accept payment in installments?

B：您能否破例接受分期付款？

S: For overseas deliveries, the payment is to be effected by l00 % confirmed irrevocable L/C.

S：對於出口訂單，我們只接受百分百保兌不可撤銷的信用狀。

B: Is there any compromised settlement, such as 50% by T/T and the balance by D/P?

B：有任何折衷的方式嗎？例如款項的百分之五十電匯付款，其餘的用付款交單的方式呢？

S: Unfortunately, L/C at sight is normal for our exports without exception. It would be difficult for us to accept other payment methods.

S：抱歉，即期信用狀為我司出口訂單的一般付款條件，沒有例外，我們很難接受其他的付款方式。

B: Well. I'll need to speak with our finance department about this.

B：那麼，我需要再與財務部門討論一下。

S: If this is the case, I will put the order on hold until you settle the payment issue.

S：如果是這樣，我會先暫緩這筆訂單，等您確定付款方式。

B: OK. I'll get back to you as soon as I can.

B：好的，我會盡速回覆您。

CHAPTER 2 付款條件和保險條件

The seller urges the buyer to open L/C.

賣方公司催促買方公司開立信用狀。

情境對話

S: Hi, Tom. <u>As we discussed on the phone previously</u>, I thought that we had made an arrangement, said payment term as L/C at sight against your P/O No. 1234.

S：您好，湯姆。如我們先前電話討論，我以為我們對付款條件已達成共識，即以即期信用狀支付單號為1234的訂單。

B: Quite so.

B：的確如此。

S: However, we haven't received the L/C up till now.

S：但是直至目前為止，我們仍未收到信用狀。

B: How long is it overdue?

B：此筆付款晚多久了呢？

S: About a week. Per the agreement, the L/C should be established one month before delivery.

S：約一週，根據合約，信用狀需在出貨前一個月開出。

B: Truly sorry, Tony. I promise to attend to the matter right away.

B：真是抱歉，湯尼。我保證立即處理此事。

S: Again, I'd like to remind you again that the beneficiary of the L/C is Best International Trade Corp, Taiwan.

S：再次提醒您，信用狀的受益人為台灣倍斯特國際貿易公司。

S: Noted. I'll further check with our finance department and make sure to open the L/C immediately. Sorry again to cause any trouble to you.

S：知道了，我會再進一步與財務部門確認，並確定會立即開出信用狀。再次抱歉造成您的困擾。

B: Never mind. We would be grateful if you could notify us of L/C number once available, so the order can be proceeded as planned.

B：沒關係，當有信用狀號碼了，請通知我司，我們將不勝感激。我們才可依原定計畫生產訂單。

關鍵字彙

✓ **installment** *n.* [ɪn`stɔlmənt] 分期付款

同義詞：partial payment

相關詞：installment plan 分期付款購物法

✓ **overseas** *adj. adv.* [`ovɚ`siz] 海外；在國外

同義詞：abroad, in foreign parts, foreign

相關詞：overseas remittance 海外匯款

✓ **compromise** *v. n.* [`kɑmprəˌmaɪz] 妥協，折衷辦法

同義詞：make mutual concessions

相關詞：compromise with sb. over Sth. 與某人就某事達成妥協

make an exception *ph.* 例外，通融

同義詞：accommodating

相關詞：everything without any exception 全部

without exception *ph.* 沒有例外

同義詞：to except no one，make no exception

相關詞：There is no rule without exception. 有規則必有例外

put on hold *ph.* 暫緩，擱置

同義詞：be in abeyance, lay aside

相關詞：put the project on hold 計畫暫緩；put everything on hold 停下手邊工作

overdue *a.* [`ovə`dju] 過期的

同義詞：late, due, past due

相關詞：overdue notices 逾期通知單；3-day overdue 過期3天

beneficiary *n.* [ˌbɛnə`fɪʃərɪ] 受益人

同義詞：recipient, beneficial owner, pensioner

相關詞：beneficial legacy 有權受益的遺產

notify *v.* [`notəˌfaɪ] 通知

同義詞：inform, advise, report

相關詞：notify Sb. of Sth. 將某事通知某人；notify a third party 通知第三方

proceed *v.* [prə`sid] 繼續進行

同義詞：progress, go forward, go ahead

相關詞：proceed no further 無進展；proceed in parallel 同時進行

attend to the matter *ph.* 處理此事

同義詞：handle the matter；deal with the matter；dispose of the matter

相關詞：a matter of great urgency 當務之急

關鍵句型

It would be difficult for us to accept ...　我們很難接受⋯

例句說明：

- **It would be difficult for us to accept** the continuing delay of shipment.
  我們很難接受出貨持續延遲。

I will put Sth. on hold until ...　我會暫緩某事直到⋯

例句說明：

- **I will put the quotation on hold until** receiving the formal inquiry sheet.
  我會暫緩報價直到收到正式詢價單。

As we discussed on the phone, ...　如我們電話中所討論的⋯

例句說明：

- **As we discussed on the phone,** the increase of order quantity is required by the customer.
  如我們電話中所討論，客戶需求增加訂單量。

We would be grateful if you could ...　如果你可以⋯我們會很感激

例句說明：

- **We would be grateful if** you would accept one-week delay of the shipment.
  如果你可以接受出貨延遲一星期，我們將不勝感激。

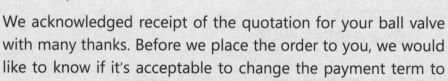

英文書信這樣寫

Inquiry of Payment Term 詢問付款條件

Dear Tony,

We acknowledged receipt of the quotation for your ball valve with many thanks. Before we place the order to you, we would like to know if it's acceptable to change the payment term to D/P at sight, as most of our suppliers dealing with us.

We look forward to your positive reply to kick off the business relation benefiting each other.

Sincerely yours,
Tom Smith

— 中文翻譯 —

湯尼 您好：

我司收到貴司球閥報價，感激不盡。下訂單給貴司之前，我們想要知道是否貴司可接受付款條件改為即期付款交單，就如同我司大部份供應商與我們交易的方式。

期盼貴司回覆，以啟動雙方互利的合作關係。

湯姆 史密斯 敬啟

Response for Payment Term 回覆付款條件

Dear Tom,

We appreciate your interest in our ball valve.

Regarding the payment term, we're sorry that we cannot accept D/P at sight. Please kindly understand that the payment term we can accept for the new customer is irrevocable L/C at sight in our favor within 14 days from the date of your order.

However, we assure you that our further business in the future will lead to a further discussion of extension of the payment terms.

We look forward to your prompt confirmation with the order.

Sincerely yours,
Tony Yang

─ 中文翻譯 ─

湯姆 您好：

感謝貴司對我司球閥的詢問。

關於付款條件，很抱歉我司無法接受付款交單的方式。請諒解我司對於新客戶僅能接受下單日十四天內以我方為抬頭的即期不可撤銷信用狀作為付款條件。不過，待日後雙方有進一步業務往來後，將進一步討論放寬付款條件。

期待儘快收到您確認下單的消息。

湯尼 楊 敬啟

信用狀開立通知

L/C Opening Notification

　　通知銀行接獲開狀銀行開來之信用狀或修改書，確認其外觀之真實性後，通知信用狀受益人前來領取。通過銀行的確認後，客戶可信任該通知信用狀之安全性，以利出貨之安排。

情境說明

The buyer notifies the seller of L/C opening.
買方公司通知賣方公司信用狀已經開立。

角色介紹
買方 | Buyer: B, ABC Co., Ltd.
賣方 | Seller: S, Best International Trade Corp.

情境對話

B: Hello, Tony. I have made an application to London bank to open the L/C in your favor to be settled in US dollars against our sales confirmation. The reference number of L/C is LB123.

B：您好，湯尼，我們已經依據銷售確認書向倫敦銀行申請開立以貴司為收益人的信用狀，會以美元結算。信用狀號碼為LB123。

S: That's great. What is the validity date

S：太好了！信用狀的有效期

of the L/C?

B: This L/C expires on May 15, 2018.

S: OK, I'll notify our finance department to further check and effect the shipment within 30 days after receiving the letter of credit.

B: I thought the batch should be released by the end of this month.

S: The production is postponed due to the delayed opening of the L/C.

B: I deeply apologize for the delay in opening the L/C. Please keep us posted of the production status to see if there's any chance to advance the shipment.

S: I don't feel too optimistic about the advance shipment but will still try our best to dispatch the products as soon as we can.

B: Appreciated. Please be reminded that our L/C is payable upon receipt of shipping documents.

到什麼時候呢？

B: 2018年5月15日到期。

S: 好的。我會通知財務部門進一步確認，並在收到信用狀30日內裝船。

B: 我以為這月底會安排出貨。

S: 因為貴司的信用狀開得太遲，造成生產延後了。

B: 深摯的抱歉延遲開狀。請隨時告知我們生產狀況，看看是否有機會提前出貨。

S: 對於提前出貨，我覺得不太樂觀，但仍會儘我們所能盡速出貨。

B: 謝謝！請注意我方的信用狀是憑裝運單據支付。

情境說明

The buyer notifies their bank to amend L/C.
買方公司通知銀行修改信用狀。

角色介紹

買方 | Buyer: B, ABC Co., Ltd.

銀行 | Bank: K, London Bank

情境對話

K: London Bank, this is Dara speaking.

K：這裡是倫敦銀行，我是姐拉。

B: Hello, Dara. This is Tom Smith from ABC Co.

B：您好，姐拉，我是ABC公司的湯姆 史密斯。

K: What can I help you with today, Mr. Smith?

K：今天有甚麼需要嗎，史密斯先生？

B: I can't succeed the online application for L/C amendment.

B：我無法成功完成線上申請修改信用狀。

K: I'm sorry. We are conducting a routine system maintenance. The online services will recommence by tomorrow morning.

K：很抱歉，我們正在進行常規系統維修，線上服務將在明天早上恢復正常運作。

B: It doesn't matter. I just faxed the Application for Amendment to Documentary Credit about 5 minutes

B：不要緊，我約在五分鐘前剛傳真了信用狀修改申請書，因為這是緊急案件，

ago. As this is an urgent case, could you please attend to this matter immediately?

你能不能立即處理這件事？

K: Please hold on and Let me check. OK, Mr. Smith, you request to increase the amount to USD3,300 and allow the transshipment with extending the latest date of shipment to June 1, 2014.

K：請稍後，我確認一下。好的，史密斯先生，您要增加信用狀金額至3300美元，允許轉運，以及最後裝船日延期至2014年6月1日。

B: That is correct.

B：沒錯。

K: No problem. I'll amend the credit accordingly.

K：沒問題，我會依此修改。

關鍵字彙

✓ **validity** *n.* [vəˋlɪdətɪ] 有效性

同義詞：availability, effectiveness

相關詞：the period of validity 有效期；validity of the assumption 假設的正當性

✓ **expire** *v.* [ɪkˋspaɪr] 期滿，終止

同義詞：become due, end, cease

相關詞：driving licence expires 駕照到期；life-expired 作廢的

✓ **effect** *v.* [ɪˋfɛkt] 生效、造成

同義詞：influence, produce, perform

相關詞：come into effect 實施；carry into effect 使生效；of no effect 無效

make an application *ph.* 申請

同義詞：apply for, ask for

相關詞：closing day for application 申請截止日；written application 書面申請

in your favor *ph.* 以你為受益人

同義詞：with you as the beneficiary

相關詞：in favor of the other party 以他方為受益人

be settled in US dollars *ph.* 以美元付款

同義詞：pay in US dollars

相關詞：pay by check 支票付款；claim payment 要求付款

conduct *v.* [kən`dʌkt] 引導，帶領

同義詞：manage, direct, lead

相關詞：conduct me 帶領我；conduct experiment 進行實驗

recommence *v.* [ˌrikə`mɛns] 重新開始

同義詞：renew, resume, begin again

相關詞：recommencement 從頭再做

documentary *a.* [ˌdɑkjə`mɛntərɪ] 文件的

同義詞：consisting of document

相關詞：documentary film 記錄片；documentary proof 書面證據

online application *ph.* 線上申請

同義詞：application through internet

解　析：網際網路的普及，使得許多商業活動亦透過網際網路進行，既快速又便利，相關詞彙有: online teaching 網路教學；online advertisement 線上廣告；online marketing 網路行銷

routine system maintenance *ph.* 常規系統維修

同義詞：routine system upkeep

相關詞：equipment maintenance 設備保養；maintainability 保養條件

關鍵句型

I apologize for the delay in ...　　對於…的耽擱，我深感抱歉

例句說明：

　　· **I apologize for the delay in** response to your inquiry.

　　對於延遲回覆您的詢價，我深感抱歉。

I don't feel too optimistic about ...　　關於…我覺得不太樂觀

例句說明：

　　· **I don't feel too optimistic about** your promotion.

　　　對於你的升遷，我覺得不太樂觀。

I can't succeed in Sth.　　無法成功完成…

例句說明：

　　· **I can't succeed** the system update.

　　我無法成功完成系統更新

Please attend to this matter immediately.　　請立即處理此事

Request of second L/C Amendment 二次修改信用狀

Dear Tom,

We're sorry to inform you that we still haven't received the amended L/C No. LB 123 with correct amount as per our request.

Besides, Owning to the delay amendment, we miss the original vessel and herein, must request to extend the date of shipment to June 1.

Your prompt attention to this matter will be greatly appreciated.

Sincerely yours,
Tony Yang

– 中文翻譯 –

湯姆 您好：

很遺憾通知貴司，我司尚未收到依要求修改為正確金額的信用狀號碼LB123。

此外，因改狀延遲，導致我司錯過原訂的船班，在此需要求您將裝船日延期至六月一日。

如您能儘早處理此事，我司不勝感激。

湯尼 楊 敬啟

知識補給
信用狀當事人與關係人

一、信用狀當事人

1. **信用狀申請人（Applicant）**：開狀申請人是向銀行提交申請書，申請開立信用狀的人，一般為進口商。
2. **信用狀開狀行（Issuing Bank）**：開狀行是應申請人（進口商）的要求向受益人（出口商）開立信用狀的銀行，一般是進口商的開戶銀行。
3. **信用狀受益人（Beneficiary）**：受益人是開狀行在信用狀中授權使用和執行信用狀並享受信用狀所賦予的權益人，一般為出口商。

二、信用狀關係人

1. **信用狀保兌行（Confirming Bank）**：保兌行是應開狀行或信用狀受益人的請求，在開狀行的付款保證之外對信用狀進行保證付款的銀行。
2. **信用狀通知行（Advising Bank）**：通知行是受開狀行的委托，將信用狀通知給受益人的銀行，一般為開狀行在出口地的代理行或分行。
3. **信用狀付款行（Paying Bank/Drawee Bank）**：付款行是開狀行在承兌信用狀中指定並授權向受益人承擔付款責任的銀行。
4. **信用狀承兌行（Accepting Bank）**：承兌行是開狀行在承兌信用狀中指定並授權承兌信用狀項下匯票的銀行。在遠期信用狀項下，承兌行可以是開狀行，也可以是開狀行指定的另外一家銀行。
5. **信用狀議付行（Negotiating Bank）**：議付行是根據開狀行在議付信用狀中的授權，買進受益人提交的匯票和單據的銀行。
6. **信用狀償付行（Reimbursing Bank）**：償付行是受開狀行指示或由開狀行授權，對信用狀的付款行，承兌行、保兌行或議付行進行付款的銀行。
7. **信用狀轉讓行（Transferring Bank）**：轉讓行是應第一受益人的要求，將可轉讓信用狀轉讓給第二受益人的銀行。一般為信用狀的通知行。

二次修改信用狀
Request of L/C Second Amendment

1. 運輸相關：啟運港、目的港或轉運港與信用狀的規定不符、允許貨物短裝或超裝與否、裝運日期過期、沒有貨物裝船證明或註明「貨裝艙面」、運費由受益人承擔，但運輸單據上沒有「運費付訖」字樣等。

2. 匯票相關：匯票付款人的名稱及地址不符、匯票出票日期不明等。

3. 商業發票相關：發票上的貨物描述與信用狀不符、發票抬頭人的名稱、地址等與信用狀不符等。

4. 包險單據相關：保險金額不足、保險比例與信用狀不符、保險單據的簽發日期遲於運輸單據的簽發日期、投保的險種與信用狀不符等。

情境說明

The seller requests the buyer to re-amend L/C.
賣方公司要求買方公司再次修改信用狀。

角色介紹

買方 | Buyer: B, ABC Co., Ltd.

賣方 | Seller: S, Best International Trade Corp.

情境對話

S: Hello, Tom. I'm calling to inform you that we are forced to postpone the shipment against your P/O No. 1234.

S：您好，湯姆，我打來是要通知您我們得要延後出貨您單號為1234的訂單。

B: Is there any problem?

B：怎麼了呢？

S: We still haven't received the amended L/C No. LB 123 with correct amount as I mentioned earlier.

S：我們仍然沒更改為正確金額的信用狀。

B: My apologies, Tony. I weren't aware of that.

B：抱歉，湯尼，我並未注意到這事。

S: Another point is the delayed amendment caused us missed the original vessel. In this case, we have to make a transshipment via Hong Kong and the latest date of shipment need to be extended to June 1.

S：還有，延遲修改信用狀導致我們錯過了原來的船班，因此，我們必須經由香港轉船，所以最後裝運日須延後至6月1日。

B: Understand. I will get right on it immediately.

B：瞭解，我會馬上處理。

S: Please keep me informed of the progress.

S：請隨時讓我知道這件事的進度。

B: I will. Sincerely apologize for our lateness on L/C amendment.

B：我會的，很抱歉我們太晚修改信用狀了。

情境說明

The seller urges the buyer to open L/C.
倍斯特公司催促ABC公司開立信用狀。

角色介紹

買方｜Buyer: B, ABC Co., Ltd.

銀行｜Bank: K, London Bank

情境對話

S: Hi, Tom. <u>As we discussed on the phone</u> previously, I thought that we had made an arrangement, and agreed on the payment term as L/C at sight against your P/O No. 1234.

B: Quite so.

S: However, we haven't received the L/C up till now.

B: How long is it overdue?

S: About a week. Per the agreement, the L/C should be established one month before delivery.

B: Truly sorry, Tony. I promise to attend to the matter right away.

S：您好，湯姆。如我們電話先前中的討論的，我們對付款條件已達成共識，即以即期信用狀支付單碼為1234的訂單。

B：的確如此。

S：但是直至目前為止，我們仍未收到信用狀。

B：晚了多久了呢？

S：約一週。根據合約，信用狀須在出貨前一個月開出。

B：真是抱歉，湯尼。我保證立即處理此事。

S: Again, I'd like to remind you again that the beneficiary of the L/C is Best International Trade Corp, Taiwan.

B: Noted. I'll further check with our finance department and make sure to open the L/C immediately. Sorry again to cause any trouble to you.

S: Never mind. We would be grateful if you could notify us of L/C number once available, so the order can be proceeded as planned.

S：再次提醒您，信用狀的受益人為台灣倍斯特國際貿易公司。

B：知道了，我會再問問財務部，確定他們會立即開出信用狀。再次抱歉造成您的困擾。

S：沒關係，當有信用狀號碼後，請通知我們，我們將不勝感激，這樣一來我們就可依原定計畫生產訂單。

關鍵字彙

- **overdue** *a.* [`ovɚ`dju] 過期的
  同義詞：late, due, past due
  相關詞：overdue notices 逾期通知單

- **beneficiary** *n.* [ˌbɛnə`fɪʃərɪ] 受益人
  同義詞：recipient, beneficial owner, pensioner
  相關詞：beneficial legacy 有權受益的遺產

- **notify** *v.* [`notəˌfaɪ] 通知
  同義詞：inform, advise, report
  相關詞：notify Sb. of Sth. 將某事通知某人；notify a third party 通知第三方

119

proceed *v.* [prə`sid] 繼續進行

同義詞：progress, go forward, go ahead

相關詞：proceed no further 無進展；proceed in parallel 同時進行

up till now *ph.* 截至目前

同義詞：up to this date, so far, up to the present

相關詞：till the end 直到最後

attend to the matter *ph.* 處理此事

同義詞：handle the matter；deal with the matter；dispose of the matter

相關詞：a matter of great urgency 當務之急

point *n.* [pɔɪnt] 要點

同義詞：keynote

相關詞：talking point 論點；selling point 賣點

amendment *n.* [ə`mɛndmənt] 改正

同義詞：revision, correction, refinement

相關詞：draft amendment 修改草案

transshipment *n.* [træns`ʃɪpmənt] 中轉；轉運

同義詞：transport, transfer

相關詞：illegal transshipment 非法轉運；transshipment trade 中轉貿易

lateness *n.* [`letnɪs] 遲；晚

同義詞：late

相關詞：lateness for work 上班遲到

latest date of shipment *ph.* 最後裝運日

相關詞：shipment date 船期；time of shipment 裝運期；date of delivery 交貨期

解　析：國際貿易實務中經常使用的裝運術語有: prompt shipment 即期裝運；
immediate shipment 立即裝運；shipment as soon as possible 儘快裝運；
shipment on or before May 15 在5月15日或之前安排裝運

✓ **get on** *ph.* 應付，處理

同義詞：proceed, progress

相關詞：get a move on 趕快；get in on supplier meeting 參加供應商會議

關鍵句型

As we discussed on the phone, ...　　如我們在電話中所討論的…

例句說明：

・ **As we discussed on the phone,** the increase of order quantity is required by the customer.

如我們電話中所討論的，客戶要求增加訂單量。

We would be grateful if you could ...　　如果你可以…我們會很感激

例句說明：

・ **We would be grateful if** you would accept one-week delay of the shipment.

如果你可以接受出貨延遲一星期，我們將不勝感激。

as I mentioned earlier　　如我先前所述

例句說明：

・ The price is too high to accept **as I mentioned earlier**.

如我先前所述，這個價格高到無法接受。

・ **As I mentioned earlier**, the function of the device is extremly good.

如我先前所述，這個裝置的功能十分出色。

Please keep me informed of Sth.　請讓我知道⋯

例句說明：
- **Please keep me informed of** your ideal price.
  請讓我知道貴司的理想價。
- **Please keep me informed of** the delivery status.
  請讓我知道裝運進度。

職場經驗談

　　遠期付款交單及承兌交單都是在進口商尚未付款之前，即可領取出貨文件辦理提貨的付款方式。一旦進口商到期拒付款，出口商即面臨極大損失，除非是長期合作且信譽良好的公司，出口商一般不會採用此付款條件，實務上來說，仍以信用狀（L/C）為主。

　　信用狀是國際貿易中使用得最普遍的付款條件，並無統一的格式，但內容基本上是相同的，大致上來說包含如下：

1. 信用狀說明：信用狀的種類、性質、編號、金額、開狀日期、有效期及到期地點、當事人的名稱和地址、信用狀可否轉讓等。
2. 匯票說明：出票人、付款人、匯票的期限以及出票條款等。
3. 貨物說明：貨物的名稱、品質、規格、數量、包裝、運輸標誌、單價等。
4. 運輸要求：裝運期限、裝運港、目的港、運輸方式、運費付款方式，可否分批裝運和中途轉運等。
5. 單據要求：單據的種類、名稱、內容和份數等。
6. 特殊條款：依據進口國政治、經濟、貿易情況，或依各別交易的差異，可做出不同的規定。
7. 信用狀當事人及關係人的相關責任文句。

　　信用狀所載內容正確與否關係著未來是否可順利議付或準時提貨，因此須審慎核對內容，務必確保與相關商業文件內容一致。

Notes 筆記欄

信用狀修改和承兌

Request of L/C Amendment and Notification of L/C Acceptance

國貿關鍵字 | 修改信用狀 |

　　信用狀分為可撤銷信用狀和不可撤銷信用狀，可撤銷信用狀是指發證行不需要經過受益人同意，可以單方面修改和撤銷的信用狀。不可撤銷信用狀是指發證行必需經過受益人同意才可以修改和撤銷的信用狀。根據信用狀分類依據的不同，信用狀還可分為可轉讓信用狀和不可轉讓信用狀、循環信用狀、對開信用狀等。

情境說明

The seller requests the buyer to amend L/C.
賣方公司要求買方公司修改信用狀。

角色介紹

買方 | Buyer: B, ABC Co., Ltd.

賣方 | Seller: S, Best International Trade Corp.

情境對話

S: Hello, Tom. This is Tony Yang from Best Corp.

B: Hi, Tony. I'm just calling to follow up the production progress against our P/O No. 1234.

S: Actually, the order is why I'm calling.

S：您好，湯姆，我是倍斯特公司的湯尼 楊。

B：您好，湯尼，我正要打電話給您追蹤訂單號碼1234的生產進度。

S：事實上，這正是我致電給

We have received your L/C No. LB123 today, but its amount is short of US$300.

您的原因。我們已經收到貴司的信用狀，號碼為LB 123，但信用狀金額短少了300美元。

B: Oh my!

B：哎呀！

S: You must amend the L/C amount to US$3,300 as soon as possible in order for as to arrange the shipment per schedule.

S：貴司必須儘速修改信用狀金額至3300美元，我們好依據能交期安排出貨。

B: How about doing it this way? You still effect the shipment as schedule and draw on us for correct amount, said USD3,300 and negotiate it under your letter of guarantee. We'll make sure to undertake your draft.

B：不如這樣做如何？貴司仍如期安排出貨，並依據正確金額開出匯票，同時出具保證書向銀行議付，我們保證如期承兌。

S: Well. This is not the mode we take usually, but we can make an exception for you this time.

S：這個嘛⋯ 這並非我們一般採用的模式，但這次我可以給個例外。

B: I truly appreciate it.

B：真的十分感謝。

The seller notifies the buyer to accept the draft against L/C.

賣方公司通知買方公司承兌信用狀所開出的匯票。

情境對話

S: Hello, Tom. It's Tony Yang from Best Corp.

S：您好，湯姆，我是倍斯特公司的湯尼 楊。

B: Hi, Tony. Nice to hear from you. What's new?

B：您好，湯尼，很高興您來電，近況如何？

S: Well, nothing much. Listen, I'm calling to advise you that your P/O No. 1234 was on board on May 29 as scheduled.

S：嗯，還是老樣子。我打來是要通知您貴司單號1234的訂單已如期在5月29日裝船了。

B: Great to hear it!

B：聽到這個消息真是太好了。

S: The copy of shipping documents were emailed to you this morning.

S：今天早上已經將出貨檔副本 email 給您。

B: Thank you. I'm going to check the papers to make sure there is no

B：謝謝您，我會檢查文件，確認是否沒有問題。

126

problem.

S: We'll draw on you for payment of the L/C amounting to $ 3,300 within one or two days. Kindly protect the draft upon presentation.

S：我們會在這一兩天內，依信用狀金額3, 300美元開出匯票給您。在匯票提示時，請予以承兌。

B: Definitely. When you send us the draft through the bank, we will accept it without delay.

B：當然，您通過銀行發出匯票時，我們將會立即予以承兌。

S: Appreciated. We will <u>arrange to deliver</u> the full set of shipping documents once receiving your bank drafts against acceptance.

S：感謝！我們一收到你方銀行承兌匯票，就會立刻安排寄出整套出貨文件。

關鍵字彙

✓ **amend** *v.* [ə`mɛnd] 修訂，修改
同義詞：change, mend
相關詞：amend the pronunciation 改正發音

✓ **negotiate** *v.* [nɪ`goʃɪˌet] 談判，協商
同義詞：settle, mediate, intervene
相關詞：negotiating table 談判桌；spinning out the negotiation 拖延談判

✓ **guarantee** *v.* [ˌgærən`ti] 保證
同義詞：promise, secure, pledge
相關詞：money-back guarantee 退款保證；guarantee for compensation 賠償保證

⊘ **mode** *n.* [mod] 模式

同義詞：manner, way, style

相關詞：operation mode 營運模式；mode of expression 表達方式

⊘ **production progress** *ph.* 生產進度

同義詞：manufacturing progress

相關詞：production priority 生產優先權；production capacity 產能

⊘ **effect the shipment** *ph.* 安排出貨

同義詞：proceed the delivery

相關詞：postpone the shipment 延遲出貨

⊘ **presentation** *n.* [ˌprizɛn`teʃən] 介紹，展示

同義詞：demonstration，exhibition, introduction

相關詞：presentation mode 展示模式

⊘ **draw** *v.* [drɔ] 開票(支票、匯票)

同義詞：write out check 開支票，draw a draft 開匯票

相關詞：blank check 空白支票；promissory note 本票

⊘ **on board** *ph.* 裝船

同義詞：put on the ship

相關詞：free on board 離岸價格；get on board 上船，登機

⊘ **protect the draft** *ph.* 承兌匯票

同義詞：honor the draft；accept the draft

相關詞：draft attached 匯票隨附

⊘ **full set** *ph.* 全套

同義詞：complete set

相關詞：full set of catalogue 整套目錄；full set of equipment 全套設備

關鍵句型

Sth. is why I'm calling.　我打來的目的正是為了…

例句說明：

- To discuss the quality problem for our last order **is why I'm calling**.
  我打來的目的正是為了討論上筆訂單的品質問題。

This is not the mode ...　並非此模式…

例句說明：

- **This is not the mode** of payment terms that our Financial Department would accept.
  這並非我們財務部門會接受的付款模式。

I'm going to .... to make sure　我將…以確定…

例句說明：

- **I'm going to** visit the supplier **to make sure** the on-time delivery of raw material.
  我將會拜訪供應商，以確定原物料可如期交貨。

We will arrange to deliver ...　我們將安排寄出…

例句說明：

- **We will arrange to deliver** the catalogue and price list within this week.
  我們將安排在本週寄出產品目錄及價格表。

Request to Amend L/C 要求修改信用狀

Dear Tom,

After reviewind to the L/C against your P/O No. 1234, we notice that there's an insufficiency in the amount.

The amount of your L/C is only USD3,000, which is USD300 shorter than the total value of your order.

Please make the L/C amendment to increase the amount to USD3300 at once to ensure the production and shipment of your order will be arranged in time.

Your prompt reply will be highly appreciated.

Sincerely yours,
Tony Yang

− 中文翻譯 −

湯姆 您好：

在檢視貴司針對訂單號碼 1234 所開出的信用狀後，發現金額不足。

貴司信用帳金額為3000美元，比訂單金額短少 300美元。

請立即請立即將信用將金額修改為3300美元，以保證能及時生產及裝運。

希望您儘速回覆，我司將感激不盡。

湯尼 楊 敬啟

知識補給

銀行信用的運作過程

第一階段 國際貿易買賣雙方在貿易合同中約定採用信用狀付款。

↓

第二階段 買方向所在地銀行申請開狀。開狀要繳納一定數額的信用狀定金，或請第三方有資格的公司擔保。

↓

第三階段 開狀銀行按申請書中的內容開出以賣方為受益人的信用狀，再通過賣方所在地的往來銀行將信用狀轉交給賣方；賣方接到信用狀後，經過核對信用狀是否符合合同條款，確認信用狀合格後發貨。

↓

第四階段 賣方在發貨後，取得貨物裝運的有關單據，按照信用狀規定，向所在地銀行辦理議付貨款。

↓

第五階段 議付銀行核驗信用狀和相關單據後，按照匯票金額扣除利息和手續費，將貨款墊付給賣方。

↓

第六階段 議付銀行將匯票和貨運單寄給開狀銀行收賬，開狀銀行收到匯票和相關單據後，通知買方付款。

↓

第七階段 買方接到開狀銀行的通知後，向開狀銀行付款贖單。贖單是指向開狀銀行交付除預交開狀定金後的信用狀餘額貨款。

寬鬆付款條件
Request of Easing Payment Terms

國貿關鍵字 ｜付款條件｜

　　通常每間公司都有固定的付款條件(Payment terms)，有時在經濟景氣不好或是買方公司周轉有問題時，買方可能會提出延長付款周期的要求。當買方提出此要求時，業務需要先知會財務部門，讓公司決定是否能夠接受這個提議，也可以留心這個警訊來判斷這家公司的財務狀況。

情境說明

The buyer ABC Co. request the seller to ease payment terms.

買方公司要求賣方公司放寬付款條件。

角色介紹

買方｜Buyer: B, ABC Co., Ltd.

賣方｜Seller: S, Best International Trade Corp.

情境對話

B: Good morning, Tony. Your draft with US$10,000 against our P/O No. 1234 was presented and duly accepted.

S: I'm just going to call you to express my appreciation for your prompt payment.

B：早，湯尼，針對我司訂單號碼1234所開出的10,000美元匯票已提示並及時承兌了。

S：我才正要打電話給您，謝謝您迅速安排付款。

B: That's what we have to do. Actually, the primary aim of my call is to discuss with you the payment terms.

S: What kind of payment terms are you considering?

B: As you know, the bank charges of opening L/C would increase our import cost side. We do hope that you can consider the payment terms as D/A or D/P.

S: Well. Seeing that we have cooperated well with each other for years, we can make exception in your favor, accepting payment term by D/P for future business.

B: Wonderful. It would help us greatly.

S: We sincerely hope to develop further mutual benefit and seek a better future.

B: It's also what we expect. Once again, really appreciate all your commitment and support.

B：這是應該的。事實上，我打電話的主要目的是要進一步商議付款條件事宜。

S：貴司想考慮哪種付款條件？

B：如您所知，銀行的信用狀開狀費會增加我們的進口成本。我們希望貴司考慮付款交單或承兌交單的付款條件。

S：好吧！有鑑於我們雙方多年來彼此合作愉快，我們可以破例接受貴司的要求，接受以付款交單作為未來合作的付款條件。

B：太好了！那真是幫了我們一個大忙。

S：我們誠摯地希望更進一步發展的雙方利益，並追求更好的未來。

B：這也是我們所期待的！再次感謝貴司的支持。

1

2 CHAPTER 付款條件和保險條件

3

4

關鍵字彙

◎ **aim** *n.* [em] 目標，目的

同義詞：purpose, intention, goal

相關詞：sole aim 唯一目標；steady aim 堅定不移的目標

◎ **cooperate** *v.* [ko`ɑpə͵ret] 合作

同義詞：collaborate, combine, concur

相關詞：cooperate perfectly 密切合作

◎ **seek** *v.* [sik] 尋找，追求

同義詞：hunt, search, pursue

相關詞：not far to seek 顯而易見；seek one's fortune 尋找成功的機會

◎ **commitment** *n.* [kə`mɪtmənt] 託付，交託

同義詞：commission, obligation, oath

相關詞：lack of commitment 未盡全力；meet the commitment 遵守承諾

◎ **bank charges** *ph.* 銀行費用

同義詞：bank fee, bank expenses

相關詞：bank borrowings 銀行借貸；bank account 銀行帳戶

◎ **import cost** *ph.* 進口成本

相關詞：import duty 進口稅，import surcharge, import surtaxes 進口附加稅

解　析：進口成本是指進口商買進商品所需支付的相關費用，主要包含商品價格、稅負等。

因此，進口成本＝商品價格×外匯牌價＋稅負＋其他費用

關鍵句型

to express my appreciation for Sth.　　針對某事致上謝意

例句說明：

- Please **express my appreciation to** your supervisor for your assistance on accelerating the production.

  針對貴司協助加快生產，請向您主管轉達我的謝意。

the primary aim of my call is to...　　我致電的主要目的是…

例句說明：

- **The primary aim of my call is to** express my appreciation for your assistance on accelerating the production.

  我致電的主要目的是要表達對貴司協助加快生產的謝意。

英文書信這樣寫

Notification of L/C Acceptance 信用狀承兌通知

Dear Tom,

We're writing to inform you that your P/O No. 1234 has been delivered on board on May 20 as scheduled Attached please find the copies of the shipping documents.

In accordance with the irrevocable L/C No. LB 123 for USD 3,300 issued by London Bank, we have valued on you at sight against this shipment. The full set of shipping documents will be sent to you once you accept the draft.

Please kindly honor the draft immediately once presentation.

Sincerely Yours,
Tony Yang

－ 中文翻譯 －

湯姆 您好：

在此通知貴司，單號為1234的訂單已如期於五月二十日裝船，請見出貨文件附本。

依據倫敦銀行開出之總額3,300美元的不可撤銷信用狀號碼LB123，我司已對此批貨開出見票即付之匯票。一經貴司承兌後，將寄出全套裝船文件給貴司。

懇請貴司於見票後立即予以承兌。

湯尼 楊 敬啟

Request of Easing Payment Term 要求寬鬆付款條件

Dear Tony,

This is to notify you that your draft on us for USD 3,300 against our order No. 1234 was presented this morning and duly accepted.

Seeing that we have cooperated well with each other for years, we propose that you accept payment term as D/P or D/A in future to decrease our importing cost.

We expect your feedback soon.

Sincerely yours,
Tom Smith

－ 中文翻譯 －

湯尼 您好：

在此通知貴司，貴司針對訂單號碼1234所開出之3,300美元之匯票已於今日上午提示，我司並已如期承兌。

有鑑於雙方多年合作愉快，我司建議貴司能接受付款之後交單或承兌交單作為未來合作的付款條件，以降低我司的進口成本。

期待儘速收到貴司回覆。

湯姆 史密斯 敬啟

匯票（Bill of Exchange）

1. Bill of Exchange（匯票）字樣
匯票上應明確標明Bill of Exchange（匯票）字樣。

2. 匯票的出票條款（Drawing Clause）
出票條款又稱為出票依據，說明匯票是依據某個信用狀的指示而開發，及信用狀開證行將對匯票履行付款責任的法律依據。

3. 匯票期限（Tenor）
匯票上必須明確表明是即期付款還是遠期付款，如果是即期匯票則為"At Sight"，如果是遠期匯票，則應填寫遠期天數。例如At 30 Days Sight，表示30天遠期。而匯票的期限一般分為以下幾種：

At sight 即期付款

At (30, 60, 90, 180...) Days after Sight: 見票後（30，60，90，180…）天付款

At (30, 60, 90, 180...) Days after Date of Issue: 出票後（30，60，90，180…）天付款

At (30, 60, 90, 180...) Days after Date of Bill of Lading: 提單的出單日期後（30，60，90，180…）天付款

4. 匯票的金額（Amount）
匯票上的金額必須寫上小寫和大寫兩種。金額為整數時，大寫金額未尾處必須加打"Only"字樣，以防塗改，小寫金額必須與大寫金額完全一致。匯票金額的幣別應和信用狀金額的幣別完全一致。

5. 利息條款（Interest Terms）
如果信用狀中規定有匯票利息條款，則匯票上必須明確載明匯票上的利息條款文句一般包括利率和計息起訖日期等內容。

6. 匯票的抬頭（Payee）
匯票的抬頭人就是匯票的收款人，在信用狀業務中，匯票的抬頭人經常為信用狀的受益人或議付行。匯票的抬頭有以下四種：

Pay to the order of Export Company (The Beneficiary)（付給信用狀的受益人的指定人）

Pay to Export Company (The Beneficiary) or order（付給信用狀的受益人或其指定人）

Pay to the order of ***BANK（付給***銀行的指定人）

Pay to ***BANK or order (付給***銀行或其指定人）

7. 出票日期和出票地點

匯票的出票日期不得遲於信用狀的有效日期，也不得遲於信用狀的最後交單期。匯票的出票地點一般為出口公司的所在地。

8. 匯票的付款人（Drawee）

在信用狀業務中，匯票的付款人一般為信用狀的償付行、付款行、承兌行、保兌行或開證行。如果信用狀中沒有明確規定匯票的付款人，則應視開證行為付款人。

9. 匯票的出票人（Drawer）

在信用狀業務中，匯票的出票人一般是信用狀的受益人，即出口公司。

10. 匯票的背書

如果匯票的抬頭是Pay to the order of Export Company (The Beneficiary)（付給信用狀的受益人的指定人）或Pay to Export Company (The Beneficiary) or order（付給信用狀的受益人或其指定人），而匯票是由信用狀的受人出具的匯票應由出票人作背書，而議付銀行寄單索匯時也作背書。

如果匯票的抬頭是Pay to the order of · ▪BANK（付給***銀行的指定人）或Pay to ***BANK or order（付給***銀行或其指定人），而匯票是由信用狀的受益人出具的，出票人不應作背書，由議付銀行寄單索匯時作背書。

託收
Application of Collection

指出口商向進口商開出匯票，透過本國託收銀行委託其國外往來銀行向進口商收取票款，可分為跟單匯票託收(Documentary Bill)，即D/P付款交單及D/A承兌交單，以及光票託收(Clean Bill)：

1.跟單匯票(Documentart Bill of Exchange)；押匯匯票：出口商開出商業匯票，將其對國進口商的債權，轉讓予外匯銀行，以出貨文件作為質押依據，或以貼現方式取得債權。

2.光票(Clean Bill)；信用匯票：出口商開出商業匯票，將其對國進口商的債權轉讓予外匯銀行，並「不」交付出貨文件及兌收現款。

情境說明

The seller applies for outward collection with bank.

賣方公司向銀行申請出口託收。

角色介紹

銀行｜Bank: B

賣方｜Seller: S, Best International Trade Corp.

情境對話

B: Good morning, Sir. What service would you like?

B：早安，先生。需要什麼服務嗎？

S: I want to apply for outward collection.

S：我想要申請出口託收。

B: Documentary collection or clean

B：跟單託收或光票託收？

collection?

S: Documentary collection and D/P.

B: Documentary collection <u>requires the draft accompanied by</u> commercial documents.

S: Here are Commercial Invoice in duplicate, full set of B/L, Packing List, and Insurance Policy.

B: Let me see. They are correct. Please fill out this application form for-outward collection. By the way, <u>you are also suggested to</u> complete this authorization form, then you can apply for trading financial service you required by fax afterwards.

S: Thanks a lot. It'd be much easier.

S：跟單託收，付款交單。

B：跟單託收要求匯票須附上商業單據。

S：這是一式兩份的商業發票、全套提單、包裝單及保險單。

B：讓我看一下…文件沒錯。請填寫這份出口託收申請表，順道一提，建議您可以同時填寫此份授權書，以後即可以傳真方式申請所需的外貿金融服務。

S：多謝！這樣方便多了。

The seller notifies the buyer to accept the draft.

倍斯特公司通知ABC公司承兌匯票。

角色介紹

買方 | Buyer: B, ABC Co., Ltd.

賣方 | Seller: S, Best International Trade Corp.

情境對話

S: Hello, Tom. It's Tony Yang from Best Corp.

S：您好，湯姆，我是倍斯特公司的湯尼 楊。

B: Hi, Tony. What's on your mind?

B：您好，湯尼，有什麼事嗎？

S: I'm calling to advise you that your P/O No. 1234 had been delivered on board on May 29 as schedule.

S：我打電話是要通知您貴司單號為1234的訂單已如期在5月29日裝船。

B: Yeah, I was aware of it.

B：是的，我注意到這個訊息了。

S: The copies of shipping documents was emailed to you this morning.

S：今天早上已經將出貨檔副本 email 給您。

B: I just got them without any problem. Thank you.

B：我剛收到文件了確認沒有問題，謝謝您！

S: Meanwhile, the draft against invoice amount USD 3,300 has been through

S：同時，依據發票金額3,300美元所開出的匯票已交由

the remitting bank on documentary collection. Please make payment against our documentary draft as soon as you can.

託收行按跟單託收，請儘速依跟單匯票付款。

B: Definitely. We will honor it without delay once receiving notification from collecting bank.

B：當然，等收到託收銀行通知後，我們會立即付款。

S: Appreciated. The bank is prepared to make the delivery of shipping document immediately on your acceptance of draft.

S：感謝！等貴司一承兌匯票，銀行就會立刻寄出正本出貨文件。

關鍵字彙

✓ **commercial document** *ph.* 商業文件
同義詞：business document
相關詞：commercial bank 商業銀行

✓ **outward collection** *ph.* 出口託收
相關詞：principal 委託人（一般是出口商），remitting bank 託收行（出口商委託代收款項的銀行），collecting bank 代收行（向付款人收款的銀行），drawee 付款人（一般是進口商）。

✓ **documentary collection** *ph.* 跟單託收
相關詞：terms and conditions of collection 託收條款
解　析：跟單託收是匯票連同出貨文件向進口商收取款項的託收方式。

⊘ **clean collection** *ph.* 光票託收

相關詞：application for collection of bills 出口託收申請書

解　析：光票託收指匯票不附加出貨文件的託收方式。

⊘ **honor** *v.* [ˋɑnɚ] 承兌

同義詞：protect, accept

相關詞：dishonor the check 拒絕承兌支票

⊘ **collecting bank** *ph.* 代收行

相關詞：principal 匯票出票人（一般指出口商）

解　析：代收行是指接受託收行的委託，向付款人（進口商）收款的進口地銀行。代收行大部分都是託收行的國外分行或代理行。

⊘ **remitting bank** *ph.* 託收行

相關詞：drawee 付款人（一般指進口商）

解　析：託收行是指接受委託人(出口商)的委託，負責辦理託收業務的銀行。託收行大部分為出口地銀行。

⊘ **documentary draft** *ph.* 跟單匯票

相關詞：documentary credit 跟單信用狀

解　析：跟單匯票又稱「信用匯票」、「押匯匯票」，為需要附帶提單、保險單、裝箱單、商業發票等商業文件才能進行付款的匯票。

關鍵句型

We will V. Sth. without delay.　我們將立即做某事

例句說明：

· **We will** kick off new production development **without delay**.
我們將立即開始開發新產品開發。

英文書信這樣寫

Request of Acceptance 要求承兌匯票

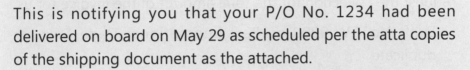

Dear Tom,

This is notifying you that your P/O No. 1234 had been delivered on board on May 29 as scheduled per the atta copies of the shipping document as the attached.

In the meantime, the draft against invoice amount USD 3,300 has been through the remitting bank on documentary collection. Please make payment against our documentary draft as soon as you can.

Thanks for your kind support to Best Corp.

Sincerely yours,
Tony Yang

－ 中文翻譯 －

湯姆 你好：

在此文通知您，貴司第1234號訂單已如期在5月29日裝船，如附件裝船文件副本所示。

同時，依據發票金額3,300美元所開出的匯票已交由託收行按跟單託收，請儘速依跟單匯票付款。

感謝貴司對倍斯特公司的支持。

湯尼 楊 敬啟

Application of Collection 申請託收

Dear Sirs,

We submit the commercial documents as listed below to request the collection for the total amount of the invoice for us.

- Draft No. TW 9900 on Best International Trade Corp. in duplicate
- Commercial Invoice No. BI 06070 for the amount of USD3,300
- Insurance Policy No. TW1122
- Full set of Clean on Board B/L No. EG 1122
- Packing-list
- Inspection Certificate
- Certificate of Original

Please drop us a message once the amount was collected.

Sincerely yours,
Tony Yang

– 中文翻譯 –

敬啟者：

我司提交下列商業文件需求貴行協助託收商業發票所載全額款項。

-第TW 9900 號匯票，受益人倍斯特國際貿易公司，一式兩份

-第BI 06070 號商業發票付款金額3,300美元，

-第TW1122 號保險單

-第EG 1122 號全套清潔提單

-裝箱單

　　-檢驗證書
　　-產地證明書
待貴行收到款項後，請通知我司。

湯尼 楊 敬啟

知識補給

跟單匯票託收流程：

1. 出口商與進口商簽署合約，同意依據跟單託收之方式收取款項。
2. 出口商安排出貨並將出貨文件及相關託收單據送交託收銀行。銀行將託收指示送交進口商銀行（代收行）。
3. 代收行通知進口商，由其決定是否付款。
4. 進口商支付款項或承兌匯票，並領取出貨文件。
5. 代收行將款項匯至託收銀行。
6. 託收銀行將款項存入出口商帳戶。

職場經驗談

　　T/T 電匯是目前實務上最省時省錢的付款方式，其流程為進口商填具匯款單，銀行依據匯款單上所載明收款人詳細資料，將款項匯付至出口商指定之銀行，即完成匯款作業，收款人約1-2天內即可收到款項，而電匯手續費約為USD10 - USD50。電匯屬預付款項的付款條件之一，一般為簽訂合約後預付一定比列款項，出貨後付清剩餘款項，或者也有少數接受在出貨後才全額支付款項，因此電匯付款就須以買賣雙方信任度為基礎。實務上來說，信用狀（L/C）仍為對買賣雙方來說最具保障的付款方式。

拒絕和延遲承兌
Refusal and Delayed of Acceptance

國貿關鍵字 | 延遲承兌

拒絕承兌，是指匯票付款人在持票人如期向其出示匯票請求表示承兌而予以拒絕的行為。亦即付款人表示於到期日不支付匯票金額的一種票據行為。

情境說明

Buyer refuses to accept the draft due to the delayed shipment by seller.

買方因賣方出貨延遲拒絕承兌匯票。

角色介紹

買方 | Buyer: B, ABC Co., Ltd.

賣方 | Seller: S, Best International Trade Corp.

情境對話

B: Hello, Tony. This is Tom Smith from ABC Co.

B：您好，湯尼，我是ABC公司的湯姆 史密斯。

S: Hey, Tom. What can I do for you?

S：嘿! 湯姆，有什麼能為您效勞的地方嗎？

B: I was surprised that you drew a bill of exchange on us for our P/O No.

B：我很驚訝貴司對我司單號5678開出匯票。

5678.

S: The shipment was effected this week. We just proceeded payment requirement as normal process.

S：該訂單已於本週出貨了，我們只是依一般流程提出付款要求。

B: The problem is that the P/O was already cancelled as you can't ensure the on-time delivery for whole batch per our request. Didn't you see my e-mail of April 20?

B：問題是因貴司無法依據我司要求確保整批貨如期出貨，此筆訂單已取消了，你沒收到我4月20日寄出的 email 嗎？

S: I've asked off for three weeks for some personal reasons and just resumed early this week. I haven't had time to go through all my e-mails yet. I'm really sorry.

S：因私人因素我請假了三週，本週才剛回來。因此還沒有時間看完所有 emails，非常抱歉。

B: Unfortunately, we had refused to accept the bill.

B：很遺憾，我司已拒絕承兌。

情境說明

Buyer requests seller to allow the delay of acceptance.

買方請求賣方接受承兌延遲。

角色介紹

買方｜Buyer: B, ABC Co., Ltd.

賣方｜Seller: S, Best International Trade Corp.

情境對話

B: Hello, this is Tom Smith from ABC Co. I want to discuss our P/O No. 1122.

B：您好！我是ABC公司的湯姆 史密斯。我想要討論我司單號1122。

S: Sure, Tom. I'm aware of that order which was already completed last month and is now under payment stage.

S：好的，湯姆，我知道這筆訂單已於上個月完成，現在已進入付款階段了。

B: Well, here is a problem. One of our main customer failed to settle our account in full because of an investment failure that caused us a serious cash-flow problem.

B：嗯，現在有一個問題。我司其中的主要客戶因投資失利，無法全額付清給我們的款項給我司，因此對我們造成嚴重的資金問題。

S: I am really sorry to hear this news.

S：很遺憾聽到這個消息。

B: I got a big favor to ask you. For the

B：我想請你幫個大忙。針對

payment of the acceptance bill against this P/O, we need you to allow us 30 days extension to resolve current financial difficulty.

此筆訂單的付款承兌匯票，我們需要貴司延期三十天，讓我們度過現階段的財務困境。

S: Well! Considering you are our best business partner with good credit, of course, <u>we are willing to</u> allow your payment of the draft to stand over per the requested period.

S：好吧！因貴司是我們信譽卓越的合作夥伴，我們願意依據貴司要求的期限，延後貴司的付款承兌。

B: Truly appreciated, Tony. You have really do me a great favor.

B：真的很感激，湯尼，您真的幫了我一個大忙。

關鍵字彙

⊘ **resume** *v.* [rɪˋzjum] 重新開始，繼續

同義詞：continue, return to, go on with

相關詞：resume production 重新投產；resume business relation 恢復合作關係

⊘ **payment requirement** *ph.* 付款要求

同義詞：payment, demends

相關詞：non-payment 未付款；the last payment 尾款

⊘ **normal process** *ph.* 一般流程

同義詞：general flow, general procedure

相關詞：project management process 專案管理過程；time-consuming process 耗時的流程

on-time delivery *ph.* 準時出貨

同義詞：on-time shipment

相關詞：express delivery 快遞；recorded delivery 掛號寄出

ask off *ph.* 請假

同義詞：absence, ask for leave, be away

相關詞：give me leave 准假；take a day off 請假一日

personal reason *ph.* 個人因素

同義詞：individual factor, personal elements

相關詞：social factor 社會因素

main customer *ph.* 主要客戶

同義詞：chief buyer, principal client

相關詞：customer satisfaction 顧客滿意度

settle the account in full *ph.* 全額結清

同義詞：pay the total payment, close off the payment, rule off the payment

相關詞：clean up old debts 結清舊債；settle up 結清

investment failure *ph.* 投資失利

同義詞：investment loss

相關詞：lack of investment 投資不足；invest in managed funds 投資管理基金

financial difficulty *ph.* 財務困境

同義詞：financial trouble, financial distress, financial squeeze

相關詞：to struggle financially 身處財務困境；financial management 財務管理

stand over *ph.* 延期

同義詞：postpone, defer, put off

相關詞：stand over until tomorrow 延至明日

關鍵句型

I am surprised that ...　　我對於…感到驚訝

例句說明：

- **I am surprised that** your offer is so high.

  我對於貴司報價如此高感到驚。

- **I am surprised that** the shipment was delayed.

  我很驚訝出貨延遲了。

The problem is that ...　　問題是…

例句說明：

- **The problem is that** your offer is much higher than our target price.

  問題是貴司的報價比我們目標價高出許多。

- **The problem is that** the shipment was delayed too long price.

  問題是出貨延遲太久了。

Of course, we are willing to ...　　我們當然願意…

例句說明：

- **Of course, we are willing to** reconsider your proposal. 我們當然願意再次考慮你的提案。

If there's anything else (that) ...　　如果還有其它事…

例句說明：

- **If there's anything else** about our company you want to know, please contact me. 如果還有其它關於我司的事項你想了解的，請與我聯絡。

Refusal of Acceptance 拒絕承兌

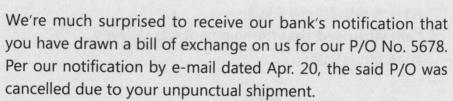

Dear Tony,

We're much surprised to receive our bank's notification that you have drawn a bill of exchange on us for our P/O No. 5678. Per our notification by e-mail dated Apr. 20, the said P/O was cancelled due to your unpunctual shipment.

Please Kindly understand that there's no reason for us to honor the draft.

Sincerely yours,
Tom Smith

— 中文翻譯 —

湯尼 您好：

我十分驚訝收到銀行通知貴司對我司第5678號訂單開出匯票。根據我司四月二十日的 email 通知，此訂單因貴司無法準時出貨已取消了。

請諒解我司拒絕承兌匯票。

湯姆 史密斯 敬啟

Delay of Acceptance 承兌延遲

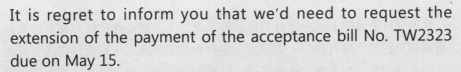

Dear Tony,

It is regret to inform you that we'd need to request the extension of the payment of the acceptance bill No. TW2323 due on May 15.

One of our main customers failed to settle our account in full owning to an investment failure, which caused us serious cash-flow problems. It will be greatly appreciated if you would allow us an extension of 30 days.

Thanks in advance for your kind understanding of our situation. Please confirm your acceptance by return, if you have no other concern.

Sincerely yours,
Tom Smith

─ 中文翻譯 ─

湯尼 您好：

很遺憾通知貴司，對已由我司承兌將在五月十五日到期的匯票，我司必須提出延期付款要求。

我司一個主要客戶因投資失利，無法全額付清貸款，因此對我們造成嚴重的資金流問題。如貴司能將付款日延長三十天，我司將不勝感激。

先感謝貴司體諒我司立場。如無其他考量，還請回覆確認。

湯姆 史密斯 敬啟

電匯付款和支票付款

Payment Terms T/T and Check

國貿關鍵字 | 電匯付款 |

電匯付款是國際上普遍通行的付款方式之一，前提條件是雙方都需在有開通電匯服務的銀行開有賬戶。電匯時，銀行會收取匯款方一定匯款費用，而收款方則無需收費。與票匯、信匯相比，電匯的速度快，費用較高，但有利於收款方快速回收貨款。

提單為承運人在目的港交貨時所需檢視的憑證，即實務上常說的「認單不認人」。因此電放申請書上面明載託運人（出口商／賣方）放棄領取提單的權利，簽署確認後即無法再向船公司領取正本提單，但仍會發副本提單（B/L Copy）。須特別注意的是若在簽發正本提單（B/L）後，才提出電放申請，此時船公司則須收回全套正本提單（B/L）後，託運人(出口商/賣方)再填寫電放申請書。

情境說明

Seller notifies buyer to remit the balance of payment by T/T.

賣方公司通知買方公司電匯餘款。

角色介紹

買方 | Buyer: B, ABC Co., Ltd.

賣方 | Seller: S, Best International Trade Corp.

情境對話

S: Hello, Tom. This is Tony Yang calling from Best Corp.

S：您好，湯姆，我是倍斯特公司的湯尼 楊。

B: Hi, Tony. What's on your mind?

B：您好，湯尼，有什麼事嗎?

S: I'm calling to advise you that your P/O No. 1234 had been delivered on board on May 29 as schedule. And the copy of shipping document was faxed to you this morning.

B: Thanks for your notification. I'll check the papers to make sure there are no documentary errors and confirm back to you.

S: If there's no problem, please remit the 70% balance against P/O amount by telegraphic transfer.

B: Definitely. Remember to inform the forwarder to telex release the B/L upon the receipt of the payment.

S: I will and thank you for reminding me again of that.

S：我致電是要通知您貴司號碼為1234的訂單已如期在5月29日裝船。並且，今天早上出貨文件副本已傳真給您。

B：感謝您的通知。我會檢視文件確認沒有文件錯誤後回覆予您。

S：如果沒有問題，請電匯訂單金額的70%餘款。

B：當然。收到款項後，記得通知貨代電放提單。

S：我會的。感謝您的再次提醒。

Seller notifies buyer to pay by check.
賣方公司通知買方公司以支票付款。

角色介紹
買方∣Buyer: B, ABC Co., Ltd.
賣方∣Seller: S, Best International Trade Corp.

情境對話

S: Hello, Tom. This is Tony Yang calling from Best Corp.

S：您好! 湯姆。我是倍斯特公司的湯尼 楊。

B: Hi, Tony. What's on your mind?

B：您好！湯尼。有什麼事嗎?

S: I'm just calling to remind you that the shipment against your P/O No. 1234 had been effected by air freight this morning to meet your urgent requirement.

S：我只是致電提醒您貴司號碼為1234的訂單已於今天早上安排空運出貨，以因應貴司的緊急需求。

B: When can I expect to receive the goods?

B：預計何時可以收到貨?

S: The estimated arrival date is May 1st.

S：預計到貨日為五月一日。

B: Great. Appreciate your assistance.

B：太好了！感謝您的幫忙。

S: From our decision at the previous call

S：如我們上次電話會議中決

conference, we would accept pay by check deducted 5 % commission of the invoice value.

議的，我司可接受發票金額扣除5%佣金的支票面額付款。

B: Correctly. The check will be sent to your attention when the shipment reaches safely.

B：沒錯！待船安全抵達，會立即將支票寄予您查收。

S: Please drop me a message once sending it off. Also, I'll send our official receipt by return to confirm the receipt of the check.

S：待寄出支票後，請通知我一聲。同樣的，收到支票後，我司會寄出正式收據作為確認。

關鍵字彙

⊘ **notification** *n.* [ˌnotəfəˋkeʃən] 通知

同義詞：notice, circular

相關詞：release the notification 發出通知；written notification 書面通知

⊘ **error** *a.* [ˋɛrɚ] 錯誤

同義詞：mistake, inaccuracy, miscue

相關詞：trial and error 嘗試錯誤法；error-free 正確無誤的

⊘ **remit** *v.* [rɪˋmɪt] 寄匯

同義詞：make a remittance, send money

相關詞：remit money 匯款，remittee 收款人

⊘ **balance** *n.* [ˋbæləns] 結餘，結存

同義詞：remaining

相關詞：account balance 帳戶餘額

⊘ **forwarder** *n.* [`fɔrwɚdɚ] 貨運代理人

相關詞：freight forwarder 運輸代理

解　析：freight forwarder / due agent 貨運代理人，簡稱貨代，是指根據委托人的要求，代辦貨物運輸業務的機構，服務項目有代理承運人向貨主攬取貨物或代理貨主向承運人辦理托運。屬於在承運人和託運人之間的運輸中間人。

⊘ **remind** *n.* [rɪ`maɪnd] 提醒，使記起

同義詞：prompt, suggest to

相關詞：remind of 使回想起

⊘ **assistance** *n.* [ə`sɪstəns] 協助，幫助

同義詞：help, support, favor

相關詞：financial assistance 財政援助；emergency assistance facility 緊急服務設施

⊘ **deduct** *v.* [dɪ`dʌkt] 扣除，減除

同義詞：subtract, withdraw, discount

相關詞：deduct interest 扣除利息；deduct tax 扣除稅款

⊘ **commission** *n.* [kə`mɪʃən] 佣金

同義詞：brokerage, brokerage charges

相關詞：agent's cut 代理人佣金

解　析：佣金是指在商業活動中的一種勞務報酬。

⊘ **estimated arrival date** *ph.* 預計到貨日

同義詞：estimated arriving date

相關詞：dispatch date, delivery date 出貨日；on board date, shipping date 裝船日

⊘ **invoice value** *ph.* 發票金額

同義詞：invoice amount

解　析：商業發票是出口商對進口商有關購買貨物相關資料及金額的憑證，發票的單價必須與信用狀上的單價完全一致，且需註明幣別及單位。

關鍵句型

remember to inform Sb. to do Sth. 　記得通知某人做某事

例句說明：

· Please **remember to inform** your Financial Department to settle the payment.
請記得通知貴司財務部門結清款項。

Thank you for reminding me again about Sth.
感謝再次提醒我某事

例句說明：

· **Thanks you for reminding me again of** settling up our account. 感謝再次提醒我結清款項事宜。

I'm just calling to remind you of ... 　我只是致電提醒您…

例句說明：

· **I'm just calling to remind you of** the deadline of placing order based on original price.
我只是致電提醒您以舊價下訂單的最後期限。

from our decision at the previous call conference ...
如我們上次電話會議中決議的…

例句說明：

· We will place a new order based on one-year forecast **from our decision at the previous call conference**.
如我們上次電話會議中決議，我們將以一年需求下訂單。

Payment Term as T/T 電匯付款

Dear Tom,

We're pleased to advise you that the shipment of your P/O No. 1234 had been effected on May 29 as schedule. please find the attached copy of shipping document.

We'll inform the forwarder to telex release the B/L, upon the receipt of the 70% balance against P/O amount by telegraphic transfer.

Shall there be any question, please feel free to let us know.

Sincerely yours,
Tony Yang

－ 中文翻譯 －

湯姆 您好：

茲通知貴司第1234號訂單已如期在5月29日出貨。請查收附件出貨文件副本。

待收到貴司電匯訂單金額的70%餘款，我司將通知貨代電放提單。

如有任何問題，請不吝告知。

湯尼 楊 敬啟

Payment as Check 支票付款

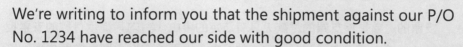

Dear Tony,

We're writing to inform you that the shipment against our P/O No. 1234 have reached our side with good condition.

In accordance with our agreement per the last phone conference, we have sent you a check for USD3,300 in payment of your invoice less 5% commission.

Please acknowledge the receipt by return.

Sincerely yours,
Tom Smith

1

2 付款條件和保險條件

3

4

– 中文翻譯 –

湯尼 您好：

以此文通知貴司，第1234號訂單的貨物已完好抵達我方。

依據我們雙方上次電話會議結果，我司已寄出面額3,300美元支票一張，以支付扣除5%佣金後之發票貨款。

請收到支票後，回覆予以確認。

湯姆 史密斯 敬啟

支票遺失和退票通知

Loss of Check and Notification for Bounced Check

國貿關鍵字 | 支票的退票 |

　　支票的退票是指支票的付款人具有法定的事由。對向其提示付款的支票拒絕付款，並將支票退還給提示付款人的行為。退票的情形主要為空頭支票、出票人簽章與預留印鑑不符的支票、欠缺法定必定紀載事項或者不符合法格式的支票、遠期支票、已經發生法律效力的支票。

情境說明

Buyer notifies the bank about the loss of check.

買方公司通知銀行關於支票遺失事宜。

角色介紹

買方 | Buyer: B, ABC Co., Ltd.

銀行 | Bank: B London Bank

情境對話

K: London Bank. This is Dara speaking.

K：這裡是倫敦銀行，我是姐拉。

B: Hello, Dara. This is Tom Smith from ABC Co.

B：您好，姐拉。我是ABC公司的湯姆 史密斯。

K: What can I help you with today, Mr. Smith?

K：今天有什麼需要嗎，史密斯先生？

B: I'm calling to request the stop payment in the check No. 11233.

B：我致電是要止付號碼為 11233的支票。

K: Is there anything wrong?

K：有什麼問題嗎？

B: This check was made out in favor of our supplier, Best Corp, but was lost during delivery. We'll draw another check to replace the missing one.

B：這張支票的受款人為我司 的供應商倍斯特公司，但 郵寄途中遺失了。我會開 出另一張支票取代遺失的 那張。

K: No problem. I'm going to deal with it at once.

K：沒問題。我現在馬上處 理。

B: Appreciated.

B：感謝！

情境說明

Seller notifies buyer about the bounced check.

賣方公司通知買方其票據退票事宜。

情境對話

S: Tom? I'm glad to run you down at last.

S：湯姆嗎？我總算找到你了。

B: What's the matter, Tony?

B：怎麼了嗎？湯尼。

S: Your check No. 445566 with US $3,300 on London Bank has bounced.

S：貴司面額3,300美金，號碼445566的倫敦銀行支票遭拒付退回。

B: Well… I'm afraid I have some bad news about the payment. We are facing severe and urgent financial shortfalls. Sincerely sorry about our late payment.

B：嗯…我恐怕要帶來一些關於付款的壞消息。我們正面臨嚴重及緊急的資金短缺。誠摯地對我司的延遲付款感到抱歉。

S: I'm really sorry to hear this news, but still need you to settle your account within this week.

S：非常遺憾聽到這個消息，但仍需求貴司須在本週內結清款項。

B: Are you able to allow us a further 90 days' grace period?

B：貴公司能否給予90天的寬限？

S: I'm not in a position to authorize your request. I'll have to talk to my CFO.

B：這個要求我無權決定。我會與財務長談談。

B: I am sorry for any inconvenience caused to you. Please keep me informed on the matter.

S：對於造成貴司的任何不便，我感到抱歉。請隨時讓我知道這件事的發展。

關鍵字彙

- ✓ **stop payment** *ph.* 止付

  同義詞：withhold payment, stop paying, suspend payment

  相關詞：continue payment 續繳；down payment 頭款

- ✓ **be made out** *ph.* 開出（支票）

  同義詞：write check, draw check

  相關詞：check stubs 支票存根；checkbook 支票簿

- ✓ **in favor of Sb.** *ph.* 以某人為受益人

  同義詞：beneficiary of

  相關詞：do Sb. a favor 幫忙；favorable treatment 優惠待遇

- ✓ **during delivery** *ph.* 運途中

  同義詞：during transportation, in transit

  相關詞：email delivery service 電子郵件傳送服務

⊘ **at once** *ph.* 立即

同義詞：immediately, promptly, right away/off /now

相關詞：all at once 突然；kick off at once 即刻展開

⊘ **bounce** *v.* [baʊns] 退票

相關詞：crossed check 劃線支票；certified check 保付支票

解　析：保付支票，是指為了避免出票人開出空頭支票，支票的收款人可要求銀行對支票保證付款，不會退票。

⊘ **severe** *a.* [sə`vɪr] 嚴重的

同義詞：strict, harsh, rough

相關詞：severe weather 氣候惡劣；severe damage 嚴重損失

⊘ **shortfall** *n.* [`ʃɔrt,fɔl] 不足

同義詞：shortage

相關詞：supply shortfalls 供應短缺；budget shortfalls 預算短缺

⊘ **grace** *n.* [gres] 寬限

同義詞：favor

相關詞：grace period 寬限期

⊘ **position** *n.* [pə`zɪʃən] 位置，職位

同義詞：post

相關詞：position of seniority 高階職位；teaching position 教職

⊘ **authorize** *v.* [`ɔθə,raɪz] 授權給

同義詞：legalize, assign, give power to

相關詞：authorized 經授權的；authorize the refund 授權退款

關鍵句型

We'll do Sth. to replace ...　　我們將做某事取代…

例句說明：

- **We'll** create a new type **to replace** the old one.
  我們會設計新款式來取代舊款。

I'm going to deal with Sth.　　我將馬上處理某事

例句說明：

- **I'm going to deal with** your urgent demand.
  我將馬上處理你的緊急需求。

Please keep me informed of Sth.　　請隨時讓我知道某事

例句說明：

- **Please keep me informed of** your final decision.
  請讓我知道你的最後決定。

I'm afraid I have some bad news about Sth.

我恐怕要帶來一些關於某事的壞消息。

例句說明：

- **I'm afraid I have some bad news about** the sorting result for the non-confirming lots.
  我恐怕要帶來一些不合格品全檢結果的壞消息。

英文書信這樣寫

Loss of Check 支票遺失

Dear Sirs,

With reference to our phone conversation today, whereby we ask you to stop paying the check No. 123.

The above-mentioned check was drawn in settlement of our account with Best International Corp., but was missed during delivery. We'll write another check to take over.

Please pay your prompt attention on this matter and ensure to stop payment of check No. 123.

Sincerely yours,
Tom Smith

一 中文翻譯 一

敬啟者

依據我們今日電話內容，在此要求您止付第123號支票。

上述支票是為了支付我司對倍斯特國際公司的欠款，但支票在郵寄過程中遺失了。我們會重新開立新票取代。

請儘速處理此事，並確保止付第123號支票。

湯姆 史密斯 敬啟

Bounced Check 退票通知

Dear Tom,

We're writing to inform you that your check No. 321 for USD3,300 on London Bank was bounced due to nonsufficient founds.

As your account still remains unpaid, please settle the full payment by T/T within one week. Otherwise, we're forced to take legal action for recovery.

Sincerely yours,
Tony Yang

－ 中文翻譯 －

湯姆 您好：

茲以此文通知貴司第321號倫敦銀行支票，票面金額3,300美元，因餘額不足遭退票。

由於貴司帳款仍未結清，請在本週內以電匯結清。否則，我們將不得不採取法律行動求償。

湯尼 楊 敬啟

1

2 付款條件和保險條件 CHAPTER

3

4

洽詢保險條件
Inquiry of Insurance Coverage

國貿關鍵字 | 保險條件 |

　　平安險(Free from Particular Average，FPA)，即承保自然災害和意外事故造成貨物的全部損失。自然災害系指惡劣氣候、雷電、海嘯、地震、洪水等，後來又加上了運輸工具遭受擱淺、觸礁、沉沒、互撞、與流冰或其他物體碰撞以及失火、爆炸造成貨物的部分損失。對裝卸、轉運時的貨物落海損失，避難港的卸貨損失，避難港、中途港的特別費用，共同海損的犧牲和分攤，以及運輸契約訂有"船舶互撞責任"條款應由貨方償還船方的損失，也包括在平安險的責任範圍內。

情境說明

Buyer inquires seller about insurance coverage.
買方公司洽詢賣方有關保險條件。

角色介紹

買方 | Buyer: B, ABC Co., Ltd.

賣方 | Seller: S, Best International Trade Corp.

情境對話

B: Hi, Tony. This is Tom Smith from ABC Co. How are you today?

B：您好！湯尼，我是ABC公司的湯姆 史密斯，今天好嗎？

S: Very well. What can I do for you, Tom?

S：很好！有什麼能幫您效勞的地方，湯姆？

B: I have received your quotation based on CIF London per our inquiry sheet. We shall give you feedback within this week.

B：我收到貴司依據我司詢價單所提供含至倫敦的運保費在內報價。我們應該會在本週內回覆給貴司。

S: That would be great. I expect your goods news.

S：太好了！期待收到您的好消息。

B: By the way, I'm wondering if you can provide more details about the coverage of the insurance.

B：順便問一下，不知道您是否可以再提供多一點關於承保範圍的細節。

S: We only cover F.P.A unless you have additional requirement, and the extra premium is to be on your account.

S：除非貴司有額外要求，我們都只投保平安險，這筆額外加保的保費須由貴司負擔。

B: At what rate against F.P.A.?

B：按什麼保險費率承保平安險呢？

S: We usually insure the goods against 110% total invoice value according to general international practices.

S：依據一般國際慣例，我們通常依發票金額的110%投保。

B: I see. Thank you.

B：瞭解。謝謝您！

情境對話

I: Taiwan Insurance Company, this is Amy speaking.

I：台灣保險公司，我是艾咪。

S: Hello, Amy. This is Tom Smith from ABC Co.

S：您好！艾咪。我是ABC公司的湯姆 史密斯。

I: Hi, Mr. Smith. How may I help you?

I：您好，史密斯 先生，需要什麼協助嗎？

S: I want to cover our shipment against All Risks. I'd like to know the details about the All Risks.

S：我想要為船貨投保全險。因此想要瞭解一下保全險相關細節。

I: To be more exact, what you required is ICC(A).

I：正確來說，你需求的會是協會貨物A條款。

S: What is its scope?

S：它的承保範圍是什麼？

174

I: "ICC (A)" covers all principal risks, but still contains some exclusion clause. I'll be glad to send you the specific extent in various risk clauses.

I： "協會貨物A條款" 包括全部主要風險，但仍有些例外。我很樂意寄給您各種險別條款的具體範圍。

S: What's the insurance rate for the cargo from HK to UK?

S： 從香港寄貨到英國的保費費率為何呢？

I: The current rate for general merchandise against the mentioned course is 0.10%. The premium will vary according to the type of goods and the circumstances.

I： 根據您所說的起迄點，目前一般貨的費率為0.10%。保險費用會因貨物類別而有所不同。

S: I see. Appreciate for your explaining.

S： 我瞭解了。感謝您的說明。

關鍵字彙

✓ **cover** *v.* [ˋkʌvɚ] 涵蓋

同義詞：include, comprise, contain
相關詞：from cover to cover 從頭到尾；cover-up 掩蓋

✓ **premium** *n.* [ˋprimɪəm] 保險費

同義詞：insurance expenses, insurance premium
相關詞：basic premium 基本保費

✓ **rate** *n.* [ret] 費率

同義詞：charge per unit, rate of pay, payment rate

相關詞：discount rate 折扣率貼現率、折現率；rated 定價格的

✓ **insure** *v.* [ɪnˋʃʊr] 為...投保
同義詞：cover, protect
相關詞：insured 已投保的；uninsured 未投保的

✓ **additional requirement** *ph.* 額外需求
同義詞：extra necessity, extra need
相關詞：basic requirement 基本需求

✓ **contain** *v.* [kənˋten] 包含；容納
同義詞：include, comprise, involve
相關詞：contain no additives 不含添加劑

✓ **exclusion** *n.* [ɪkˋskluʒən] 排除在外
同義詞：keeping out, leaving out
相關詞：inclusion 包含；exclusion zone 禁止區

✓ **specific** *a.* [spɪˋsɪfɪk] 具體的
同義詞：concrete, definite
相關詞：specific category 特定範疇；specific performance 強制履行

✓ **extent** *n.* [ɪkˋstɛnt] 範圍
同義詞：range, scope
相關詞：extent of amendment 修正範圍

✓ **circumstance** *n.* [ˋsɝkəmˌstæns] 情況
同義詞：condition, situation, state
相關詞：accidental circumstance 偶然的事；rare circumstance 不太可能的事

關鍵句型

We only ... unless ...　　我們只⋯ 除非⋯

例句說明：

- **We only** offer based on FOB term, **unless** you have different instructions.

  我們只提供離岸價，除非你另有指示。

I'm wondering if you can provide more details about Sth.

不知道您是否可以再提供多一點關於某事的細節。

例句說明：

- **I'm wondering if you can provide more details about** the re-working process of defect products.

  不知道您是否可以再提供多一點關於不良品重工的細節。

To be more exact, ...　　更確切的說，⋯

例句說明：

- **To be more exact**, your offer is twice as much as our target price.

  更確切來說，您的報價比我司目標價高出一倍。

will vary according to ...　　將依據⋯而有所變動

例句說明：

- The material price **will vary according to** the spot rate.

  原料價格會因即期匯率而有所變動。

Enquiry to Insurance Risks (from Buyer)
洽詢保險條件（買方詢問）

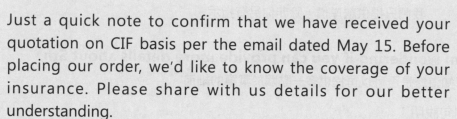

Dear Tony,

Just a quick note to confirm that we have received your quotation on CIF basis per the email dated May 15. Before placing our order, we'd like to know the coverage of your insurance. Please share with us details for our better understanding.

We hope to hear from you soon.

Sincerely yours,
Tom Smith

— 中文翻譯 —

湯尼 您好：

在此只是簡單的確認我司已收到您根據五月十五日 email 提到含運保費的報價。
在下單前，我司想要瞭解您的保險涵蓋的範圍，還請提供明細，讓我司瞭解。
希望儘快收到您的回覆。

湯尼 史密斯 敬啟

Response about Insurance Risks (from Seller)
回覆保險條件（賣方回覆）

Dear Tom,

We're writing in response to your requirement of insurance details. For the quotation on CIF basis, we usually cover the insurance against ICC (C) for 110% of the total invoice value.

If you'd like to cover the shipment against additional risks, the extra premium must be absorbed by your side.

We expect to receive your order soon.

Sincerely yours,
Tony Yang

－ 中文翻譯 －

湯姆 您好：

在此回應您所要求的保險明細。針對含運保費的報價，我司通常依商業發票金額的110%投保協會貨物C條款。

如您欲對此批貨投保附加險，則額外費用需由您負擔。

期待儘早收到您的訂單。

湯尼 楊 敬啟

職場經驗談

　　航空運輸貨物保險主要也分為「航空運輸險」和「航空運輸全險」兩種，而除外責任與海洋運輸貨物保險的除外責任相同。其責任起訖點，簡單來說就是被保險貨物運離起運地到送達目的地貨交收貨人為止（起訖地以保單為依據）。另外，航空保險也可追加戰爭險等附加險，此點亦與海洋運輸貨物保險相同。

需求額外保險和通知投保險種

Request of additional insurance and Notification of insurance risks

國貿關鍵字 | 貨物保險 |

　　實務上投保行為需在運送風險發生前辦理，因進出口業務之不同而區別如下：1 出口業務：應在向船公司/航空公司簽訂裝貨單（S/O）及辦理報關時，同時申辦保險。可先將要保書送交保險人，而後再補齊相關資料。2 進口業務：進口商應在申請輸入許可證或開發信用狀時，同時申辦保險，務必確保在啟航前投保，而保險人不負責在保險單簽發前所發生之任何損失賠償。

情境說明

The buyer requests the seller to arrange additional insurance.

買方公司需求賣方公司投保額外保險。

角色介紹

買方 | Buyer: B, ABC Co., Ltd.

賣方 | Seller: S, Best International Trade Corp.

情境對話

B: Hello, this is Tom Smith from ABC Co. I'm looking for Tony Yang, please.

B：您好！我是ABC公司的湯姆 史密斯。我找湯尼 楊，麻煩您。

S: Speaking. How are things, Tom?

S：我是湯尼。湯姆，最近可好？

B: Pretty Well. Listen, with reference to

B：還不賴。聽著，關於我們

our telephone conversation yesterday, we need you to effect insurance against ICC (C) at 110% of full invoice value against our P/O No. 2233.

昨天在電話中的談話，我們需要貴司依據第2233號訂單的發票全額的110%投保協會貨物C款險之外的險種。

S: What additional risks do you request?

S：貴司需要的額外險種為何？

B: Please increase the coverage with T.P.N.D for this consignment at our cost.

B：請為此批貨加保提貨不著險，由我司負擔保費。

S: No problem. I'll work on it today and the insurance policy shall be available by June 7.

S：沒問題。我會在今天處理，預計在六月七日前可拿到保險單。

B: We will engage the duly payment upon the receipt of the relevant insurance document and debit note for the extra premium. Thank you.

B：待收到相關保險文件及額外保費的欠款單後，我們保證會及時付款。感謝您！

S: My pleasure. Is there anything else?

S：這是我的榮幸。還有其他需要嗎？

B: No, that's it.

B：沒有了，就這樣。

Buyer notifies insurance company about the required insurance risk.

買方公司通知保險公司有關欲投保的險種。

情境對話

I: England Insurance Co, this is Annie speaking.

I：英格蘭保險公司。我是安妮。

B: Hello, Annie. This is Tom Smith from ABC Co.

B：您好！安妮。我是ABC公司的湯姆 史密斯。

I: Hi, Mr. Smith. How may I help you today?

I：您好，史密斯 先生，今天需要什麼協助嗎？

B: Yes, Annie. I just faxed the Insurance Slip for our consignment against all risks for ICC (B).

B：是的，安妮。我剛傳真託運品的投保單，投保協會貨物B款險。

I: Mr. Smith. Let me pull up your information. Yes, here it is. The consignment of industrial valves is scheduled to ship from HK to UK via S.S "Ever Lmbent." The required insured amount is US$10,000.

I：史密斯 先生。讓我找一下貴司的資料。有的，找到了。這批工業閥門託運貨預計經由"Ever Lmbent"號從香港運送至英國。所需的投保金額

182

為10,000美元。

B: Correct. But we'd like to change the insurance to ICC (A).

B：沒錯。但我想要將投保險種變更為協會貨物A款險。

I: That is alright. Just fill in the Endorsement Application Form by return.

I：沒問題。只要填回保險批改申請書即可。

B: Please proceed the application process and I'm certain that you'll receive it within 10 minutes.

B：請進行申請流程，我保證您在十分鐘內會收到申請書。

I: That should be alright. You can rely on me to give your application with immediate attention. And the Certificate of Insurance follows as soon as I receive it.

I：應該沒問題。您的訂單我將會馬上處理，請放心。一旦接到保險憑證，隨後寄給您。

關鍵字彙

⊘ **consignment** *n.* [kən`saɪnmənt] 託付物，委託貨物

同義詞：cargo, load, shipment

相關詞：consignment note 發貨通知；consignment sales 寄售

⊘ **relevant** *a.* [`rɛləvənt] 有關的

同義詞：corresponding

相關詞：irrelevant 無關的；relevant information 有關訊息

⊘ to effect insurance *ph.* 投保

同義詞：to cover insurance , to arrange insurance , to take out insurance

相關詞：declinature 拒保

解　析：拒保是指保險人對投保人及被保險人之初次投保或續保，予以拒絕承保之行為。

⊘ insurance document *ph.* 保險文件

相關詞：insurer 保險人；insured 被保險人

解　析：保險文件是保險人對被保險人的承保證明、雙方權利義務的契約，以及被保險人索賠和保險人理賠的主要依據。

⊘ increase coverage *ph.* 加保

同義詞：extend coverage

相關詞：insurance agent, insurance broker 保險代理人

⊘ T.P.N.D *n.* 偷竊、提貨不著險

解　析：Theft，Pilferage And Non-delivery 偷竊、提貨不著險是海洋貨物運輸保險普通附加險之一，其承保範圍為保險貨物被偷走或竊走，以及保險貨物運抵目的地以後，整批未交的損失，由保險人負責賠償。

⊘ pull up *ph.* 取出

同義詞：take out, draw out, pull out

相關詞：pull up the customer list 找出客戶清單

⊘ endorsement *n.* [ɪn`dɔrsmənt] 背書；簽署

同義詞：signature on a check, confirmation on a check

相關詞：blank endorsement 不記名背書

⊘ insured amount *ph.* 保險金額

同義詞：insurance amount

相關詞：insurance premium 保險費

關鍵句型

... with reference to our telephone conversation
關於我們在電話中的談話…

例句說明：

· We'll place an order for the items **with reference to our telephone conversation**.
我們會依據電話中所談的品項下訂單。

engage Sth. upon receipt of ...　待收到…後，會保證某事

例句說明：

· We'll **engage** the immediate shipment **upon the receipt of** your payment.
待收到貴司款項後，我會保證安排立即出貨。

I'm certain that ...　我確定…

例句說明：

· **I'm certain that** our offer is more favorable than the competitor's.
我確定我們的報價比起競爭者的優惠。

You can rely on me to V ...　你可以信任我…

例句說明：

· **You can rely on me to** inspect the product according to your specification.
你可以信任我會依據貴司的標準檢驗產品。

Request of Additional Insurance (from Buyer)
請求額外保險（買方需求)

Dear Tony,

With reference to our P/O No. 2233 for 1,000pcs of ball valve placed on C&F basis, please arrange ICC (A) insurance for us at 10% of the total invoice value, which is USD5,000. The premium will be paid by us upon the receipt of the relative insurance documents from you.

If you have any further questions, please feel free to let me know.

Sincerely yours,
Tom Smith

– 中文翻譯 –

湯尼 您好：

關於我司第2233號訂單，依運費在內條件訂購貴司1,000件球閥，請協助替我司依據商業發票的110%，總額50,000美元票，投保協會貨物A款險。待收到貴司提供的相關保險憑證後，我司將會支付保費。

如有任何進一步問題，請不吝告知。

湯姆 史密斯 敬啟

Request of Additional Insurance (Response from Seller)
請求額外保險（賣方回覆）

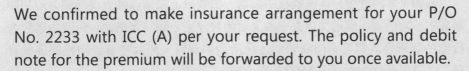

Dear Tom,

We confirmed to make insurance arrangement for your P/O No. 2233 with ICC (A) per your request. The policy and debit note for the premium will be forwarded to you once available.

The shipment will be effected on June 7. The full set of shipping document including cleaned on board B/L, Packing List, Certificate of Original, Inspection Certification as well as Commercial Invoice will be sent to you upon the receipt of your payment.

Shall there be any question, please feel free to let us know.

Sincerely yours,
Tony Yang

－ 中文翻譯 －

湯姆 您好：

我司確認已依據貴司要求為貴司第2233號訂單安排協會貨物A款險。待收到保險單及欠款單後，將轉寄貴司。

該批貨物將於六月七日出貨，全套出貨文件包括清潔裝船提單、包裝單、原產地證明書、檢驗報告及商樣發票將待收到貴司付款後寄予貴司。

如有任何問題，請不吝告知。

湯尼 楊 敬啟

提出索賠通知和請求代理索償
Notification of Claim and Request to Make Claim on Sb's Behalf

國貿關鍵字 | 缺 |

假如不幸的貨物在運送過程中損壞，需要馬上聯繫保險公司詢問索賠相關事宜，一般而言，索賠文件之一的索賠函並無固定和特定格式，只要內容包含貨物的詳細資料即可，但需特別注意所列的資料，無論是貨物明細和運輸資料，必須與商業文件，特別是信用狀一致。

情境說明

The seller notifies insurance company about the claim application.

賣方公司通知保險公司有關索賠申請事宜。

角色介紹

保險公司 | Insurance company：I, Taiwan Insurance Company

賣方 | Seller: S, Best International Trade Corp.

情境對話

I: Taiwan Insurance Co, this is Amy speaking.

I：台灣保險公司。我是艾咪。

S: Hello, Amy. This is Tony Yang from Best Co.

S：您好！艾咪。我是倍斯特公司的湯尼楊。

I: Hi, Mr. Yang. How may I help you today?

I：您好，楊先生，今天需要什麼協助嗎？

S: Yes, our consignment was found with damage upon arrival at destination per the inspection report from the local Commodity Inspection Bureau. We'd lodge a claim with your company according to our insurance risk against ICC (A).

I: OK, Mr. Yang. Let me pull up your information. Please give me the number of your Insurance Certificate.

S: The number is 88990.

I: Yes, here it is. The consignment was scheduled to ship from HK to UK via S.S "Ever Lmbent." The insured amount is USD$10,000.

S: That's correct.

I: To apply for the insurance claims, the documents needed to be prepared are the Claim List, Inspection Certificate, S/L, Invoice and Packing List.

S：是的。根據當地商品檢驗局出具的驗貨報告，我司的貨物到達目的港時被發現已損壞。我們依據投保的協會貨物A款險向貴司提出賠償。

I：好的，楊先生。讓我找一下貴司的資料。請給我您的保險憑證號碼。

S：號碼是 88990。

I：有的，找到了。這批貨經由 "Ever Lmbent" 號從香港運送至英國。投保金額為10,000美元。

S：沒錯。

I：申請保險理賠需準備的文件有索賠函、檢驗證明書、提單、商業發票及包裝單。

情境說明

The buyer requests the seller to make claim on ABC's behalf.

買方公司請求賣方公司代理賠償

角色介紹

買方 | Buyer: B, ABC Co., Ltd.

賣方 | Seller: S, Best International Trade Corp.

情境對話

S: This is Tony Yang. What can I do for you?

S：我是湯尼 楊。有什麼能為您效勞的？

B: Hello, Tony. It's Tom Smith from ABC Co. There's a problem with the goods against our P/O No. 2233.

B：您好！湯尼。我是ABC公司的湯姆 史密斯。我們第2233號訂單這批貨有問題。

S: What's wrong?

S：有什麼不對嗎？

B: 151pcs out of 2,000pcs were damaged.

B：這2,000件的產品中有151件損壞。

S: How come? <u>What sort of damage are you referring to?</u>

S：怎麼會？您所提的是哪種損壞？

B: They were found with severe scratches and abrasions on the part surface.

B：我們發現產品表面有嚴重的刮傷及擦傷。

S: Sounds bad.

S：聽起來很糟。

B: As the insurance was arranged by your side, please lodge a claim with the insurance company for us.

B：所有的保險透過貴司投保，請協助我們向保險公司提出索賠。

S: That goes without saying. I will help to handle it at once after receiving the survey's report and Broken and Damaged Cargo List.

S：那是當然的。待受到檢驗報告及貨物殘損單後我會協助立即處理。

B: Thanks a lot.

B：多謝！

關鍵字彙

✓ **certificate** *n.* [sə`tɪfəkɪt] 證明書

同義詞：certification, documentation

相關詞：Certificate for Marin Products 船用產品檢驗證書；Certificate of Clearance 出港許可證

✓ **inspection report** *ph.* 檢驗報告

相關詞：investigation report 調查報告；Customs inspection 海關查驗

解　析：查驗是進口貨物通關的重要環節，是指海關依法為確定進出境貨物內容是否與申報內容相符，對貨物進行實際的核查，確定單貨、證貨是否相符，有申報不實等行為，並為今後的徵稅、統計和後續管理的依據。

⊘ **Commodity Inspection Bureau** *ph.* 商品檢驗局

相關詞：import-export commodity inspection 進出口商品檢驗

解　析：商品檢驗局/機構，又稱「商檢局」，是指根據客戶的委託或有關法律法規的規定對進出境商品進行檢驗檢疫、鑒定和管理的機構，在國際上商品檢驗機構分為官方機構、私人機構，或同業公會經營之機構。

⊘ **insurance claim** *ph.* 保險索賠

相關詞：insurable interest principle 保險利益原則

解　析：保險索賠是指被保險人在保險標的遭受損失時，依據保險單有關條款向保險人要求賠償的行為。

⊘ **scratch** *n.* [skrætʃ] 刮痕

同義詞：scrape, mark, cut

相關詞：scratch hardness test 刮傷硬度測試；scratch marks 刮痕

⊘ **abrasion** *n.* [əˋbreʒən] 磨損

同義詞：excoriation

相關詞：abrasion resistant 耐磨；abrasion-test 耐磨測試

⊘ **lodge a claim** *ph.* 提出索賠

同義詞：to raise a claim, to make a claim, to register a claim

相關詞：claims agent 索賠代理人；claim note 索賠單

⊘ **part surface** *ph.* 產品表面

同義詞：product appearance, part outside, part cosmetic face

相關詞：part internal structure 產品內部結構；part geometry 產品外觀形狀

⊘ **Broken and Damaged Cargo List** *ph.* 貨物殘損單

解　析：貨物殘損單指是指卸貨完畢後，理貨員根據卸貨過程中發現的貨物破損、水濕、水漬、滲漏、黴爛、生鏽、彎曲變形等情況記錄編製的，證明貨物殘損情況的單據。貨物殘損單必須經船方簽認。貨物殘損單，是證明到港船舶卸貨時所交接貨物實際情況的單證，也是日後收貨人向船公司提出索賠的原始資料和依據。

關鍵句型

be found with Sth. upon ... 　在…時發現某事物

例句說明：

· Two pallets **were found with** damage **upon** the uploading.
在卸櫃時發現有兩只棧板損壞。

To apply for A, B needed to be prepared ... 　申請A，需要準備B

例句說明：

· **To apply for** video conference with customer, the information **needed to be prepared** is IP address of customer to set up the connection.
申請與客戶視訊會議，需要準備的資訊為客戶的網路位址，以做連線設定。

What sort of Sth. are you referring to? 　你所提及的是哪種…

例句說明：

· **What sort of** laptop model **are you referring to**?
你所提及的筆電機型是哪種?

to make a claim with (against) Sb. 　向某方提出索賠

例句說明：

· The consignee should **make a claim** immediately for the lost lots **with** the insurance company.
收貨人應立即向保險公司提出貨物遺失索賠。

Request to Make Claim on Sb.'s Behalf 請求代理索償

Dear Tony,

This is to inform you the shipment via S.S "Ever Lmbent" already arrived at London, but was found with severe cosmetic defect by insurance surveyors.

As the insurance was covered at your side, please take up the claim for us with the insurance company on the receipt of the surveyor's report and Broken and Damaged Cargo List.

Appreciate your kind assistance.

Sincerely yours,
Tom Smith

– 中文翻譯 –

湯尼 您好：

茲此文通知貴司，由 "Ever Lmbent" 號承運的貨物已運抵倫敦，但保險驗貨員發現貨物有嚴重的外觀不良。

由於該保險由貴司承辦，待收到檢驗報告及貨物殘損單時，請協助我方向保險公司提出索賠

感謝貴司協助。

湯姆 史密斯 敬啟

Claim Notification 提出索賠通知

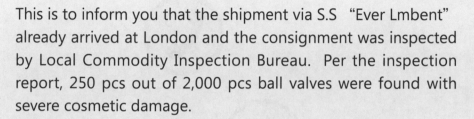

Dear Sirs,

This is to inform you that the shipment via S.S "Ever Lmbent" already arrived at London and the consignment was inspected by Local Commodity Inspection Bureau. Per the inspection report, 250 pcs out of 2,000 pcs ball valves were found with severe cosmetic damage.

Herein we lodge a claim for the mentioned damage, and request you indemnify the sum of US$565 for the damaged ones according to our insurance against ICC (A). You may refer to the detailed Lists of Claim and relative commercial documents as attachment.

Your prompt settlement will be greatly appreciated.

Sincerely yours,
Tony Yang

－ 中文翻譯 －

敬啟者：

茲此文通知貴司，由 "Ever Lambent" 號承運的貨物已運抵倫敦，並經商品檢驗局檢驗。根據檢驗報告，2,000件球閥中有250件有嚴重外觀損傷。

我方在此依據所投保的協會貨物A款險，向貴司提出索賠，折合為565美元。請參閱附件索賠清單及相關商業單據。

望貴司儘早償付我司，我司感激不盡。

湯尼 楊 敬啟

Chapter
3

交貨條件

Shipping Terms

洽詢運費和船班

Inquiry of Shipping Cost and Shipping Schedule

國貿關鍵字 | 國際運費比較 |

　　一般來說，運費和報價是分開計算。建議賣方運費可以多做比較，因為每間貨運公司或是快遞強項不同，不同運輸公司專攻不同地區，例如歐洲線和美國線。

情境說明

Seller inquires about freight rate and sailing schedule with shipping company.

賣方公司向船公司洽詢運費及船期。

角色介紹

船公司 | Shipping company : C Evergreen Marine Corp.

賣方 | Seller: S, Best International Trade Corp.

情境對話

C: Evergreen Marine Corp., this is David speaking.

S: Hello, David. This is Tony Yang from Best Co.

C: Hi, Mr. Yang. What can I do for you?

C：這裡是長榮海運，我是大衛。

S：您好！大衛。我是倍斯特公司的湯尼 楊。

C：您好，楊先生。有什麼能為您效勞的地方？

S: We have an order with around 200 tons, planned to ship in bulk from HK to London, UK. Could you provide your best freight rate and sailing schedule?

S：我司有一批200噸的貨，計畫以散裝的方式由香港運送至英國倫敦。可以提供貴司最優惠的運費及船期嗎？

C: No problem. The Liner freight tariff based on weight ton and sailing schedule will be faxed to you later.

C：沒問題。依重量噸計算的班輪運價表及船期稍後會傳真給您。

S: Thanks a lot.

S：多謝。

C: One more thing, as the recent unexpected strike caused congested Port of London, we will charge Port Congestion Surcharge against 5% of freight rate.

C：還有一件事，因為最近發生罷工造成倫敦港擁擠，我們會另收運費5%的港口擁擠附加費。

S: I see and will confirm the vessel we prefer once we decided.

S：我了解了，待確定後我會確認所要的航班。

Seller inquires about shipping schedule with shipping agency.

賣方公司向船務代理洽詢船期。

角色介紹

船務代理 | Shipping Agency: A, S&Y Shipping Agency

賣方 | Seller: S, Best International Trade Corp.

情境對話

A: S&Y Shipping Agency, this is Emma speaking.

A：這裡是S&Y船物代理，我是艾瑪。

S: Hello, Emma. This is Tony Yang from Best Co.

S：您好！艾瑪。我是倍斯特公司的湯尼 楊。

A: Hi, Mr. Yang. How may I help you?

A：您好，楊 先生，需要什麼協助嗎？

S: Here is the thing. We plan to transfer aging brass bar from Taiwan plant to Mainland plant within next half year by time charter.

S：是這樣的，我們計畫在未來半年內，以定期租船將庫齡銅材由台灣工廠轉至大陸工廠。

A: What's your estimated shipping date of the first batch?

A：首批貨的預計出貨日為何？

S: No later than June 10 from Keelung Port to Shanghai.

S：會在於六月十日前，由基隆港運至上海。

A: The required capacity is …?

A：需求的運載量呢？

S: Around 5,000 tons.

S：約5,000噸。

A: OK, What you've required has been written down. And I'll find out the suitable ship and get back to you soon.

A：好的，您需要的我都已經記錄下來了。我會找出適合的船班後儘速回覆給您。

S: Thank you.

S：謝謝您！

關鍵字彙

⊘ **bulk** *n.* [bʌlk] 散裝

相關詞：bulk cargo 散裝貨；bulk cargo container 散裝貨貨櫃

解　析：散裝運輸是指貨物不加以包裝，原則上以自然形態裝載運送，適用於大宗的塊狀、粒狀、粉狀以及液態貨物的運輸。

⊘ **strike** *n.* [straɪk] 罷工

同義詞：go on strike

相關詞：strike pay 工會在罷工期內給工人的津貼

⊘ **congested** *a.* [kənˋdʒɛstɪd] 擁擠的

同義詞：overcrowded, overloaded, stuffed

相關詞：heavily congested 十分擁擠的；congested traffic 交通擁擠

⊘ **freight rate** *ph.* 運費率

同義詞：transportation expenses, fare, carriage 運費

相關詞：ocean freight 海運；air freight 空運；land carriage 陸運

⊘ **Liner freight tariff** *ph.* 班輪運價表

相關詞：basic freight rate 基本運費率

解　析：班輪運價表是指依據班輪運輸條件所制定的不同航線、貨種或貨物等級的運費率。

⊘ **weight ton** *ph.* 重量噸

相關詞：freight ton 運費噸

解　析：運費噸是重量噸和體積噸的統稱。

　　　　1 重量噸：是按毛重（gross weight）計算，以每公噸（1000公斤）、每長噸
　　　　（1016公斤）或每短噸（907.2公斤）為一個計算運費的單位，用W表示。

　　　　2 體積噸：是按尺寸（measurement）計算，以每立方米（約合35.3147立方英
　　　　尺）或40立方英尺為1尺碼噸或容積噸，用M表示。

⊘ **transfer** *v.* [træns`fɚ] 調動

同義詞：pass, hand over, sign over

相關詞：transfer conveyor 轉載輸送機；transfer gate 輸送門

⊘ **estimated shipping date** *ph.* 預計裝船日

同義詞：on board date

相關詞：shipping clerk 理貨員；shipping company 運輸公司

⊘ **capacity** *n.* [kə`pæsətɪ] 容量，容積

同義詞：size, volume, content

相關詞：capacity factor 利用率；capacity loading 裝載量

⊘ **find out** *ph.* 找出，發現

同義詞：discover, learn about, get information about

相關詞：find out secrets 找出機密；find out the truth 找出真相

關鍵句型

We have an order of ...　我們有一批…的訂單

例句說明：

· **We have an order of** 10 sets of laptops with a computer company.

我們向一家電腦公司訂10台筆電。

will confirm Sth. (which) Sb. prefer once ...

待…後，將會確認某人所要的某事物

例句說明：

· I **will confirm the** color of laptop **which** my customers **prefer once** receiving their oral message.

待收到客戶的口頭訊息後，我將會確認所要的筆電顏色。

What you've required has been written down.

您所需要的都已記錄下來了。

職場經驗談

「船務公司」是指獨立營運且有自己船隻的公司，如長榮海運，陽明海運、或萬海海運。「船務代理公司」沒有自己的船隻，但代理多家船公司的攬貨業務。實務上船務代理能提供更多船舶資訊，服務範圍也較廣。

舉例來說，如果預計目的地為航程較少的點，洽詢單一船公司未走該點航程，船公司就無法再提供進一步協助，但若轉由船務代理，其可協助整合其他船公司的船期資料，找到可行方案。

英文書信這樣寫

Inquiry of Shipping Cost by Exporter 洽詢運費（出口商詢問）

Dear Sirs,

We have received an order for 200 Metric tons of brass, which should be shipped in bulk during this month from HK to Port of London. Please provide your best freight rate and sailing schedule.

Please respond at your earliest convenience.

Sincerely yours,
Tony Yang

— 中文翻譯 —

敬啟者：

我司收到一張200噸銅的訂單，預計在這個月安排散裝由香港運送至倫敦港，請提供貴司最優惠的費率及船期表。

請儘速回覆。

湯尼 楊 敬啟

Response of Shipping Cost by Shipping Company
洽詢運費（船公司回覆）

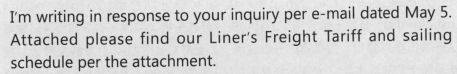

Dear Tony,

I'm writing in response to your inquiry per e-mail dated May 5. Attached please find our Liner's Freight Tariff and sailing schedule per the attachment.

Kindly be noted that the freight of bulk cargo will be calculated based on its weight. Besides, owing to the fact that the recent unexpected strike caused congested Port of London, we will charge 5% of freight as Port Congestion Surcharge. The shipment arrangement will be done as soon as you firm up the vessel.

Please let me know if there is anything I can do for you.

Sincerely yours,
David Wu

－ 中文翻譯 －

湯尼 您好：

在此回應貴司五月五日來信詢問一事。請見我司包輪運費表及船期表如附，請查看。

請注意散裝貨物將依重量計算，此外，有鑑於最近不預期的罷工，造成倫敦港擁擠，我們會另收運費5%的港口擁擠附加費，待貴司確認船班後，我方將儘速安排裝船事宜。

有任何我方能提供協助的地方，請不吝告知。

大衛 吳 敬啟

分批裝運和轉船
Partial shipments and transshipment

國貿關鍵字 | 分批裝運 |

　　分批裝運(Partial Shipment)，又稱分期裝運(Shipment by Installment)，是指一筆合約下的貨物先後分若干批次裝運。有下列情形將會無法一次出全部的貨，而須安排分批裝運：1.受訂單量限制(如訂單數量較大，無法及時全數完成生產)2.受運輸條件限制(如直達船班少)3.市場銷售限制4.資金條件限制

情境說明

The buyer requests the seller to arrange partial shipments.

買方公司要求賣方安排分批裝運。

角色介紹

買方 | Buyer: B, ABC Co., Ltd.

賣方 | Seller: S, Best International Trade Corp.

情境對話

S: Tony Yang Speaking.

S：我是湯尼 楊。

B: Hi, Tony. This is Tom Smith from ABC Co. I need a favor from you about our P/O No. 1357.

B：您好！湯尼。我是ABC公司的湯姆 史密斯。我們的第1357號訂單需要您提供協助。

S: What can I help you with, Tom?

S：需要我如何協助呢湯姆？

B: The goods is urgently required by our customer. Is it possible to process the shipment more promptly?

B：我司的客戶急需要此批貨提前交期？

S: I'm afraid that we have difficulties in meeting your requirement, as the production hasn't finished completely.

S：您的要求恐怕有困難，因為還未全部完成生產。

B: What's the available quantity now?

B：目前有多少數量？

S: We have only 200pcs on hand.

S：我們現在只有約200件。

B: Please make a partial shipment for the said quantity by express delivery in freight collect.

B：請以快遞運費到付的方式，先安排分批出現有的數量。

S: No problem. I'll arrange the shipment at once and send you the shipping details.

S：沒問題，我會立即安排出貨，並提供出貨明細給您。

情境說明

Sellers requests buyers to allow the transshipment.

賣方要求買方同意轉船。

情境對話

B: Tom Smith Speaking.

S: Hello, Tom. This is Tony Yang from Best Corp. I'm afraid we have some difficulties in transport arrangement against your P/O No. 1357.

B: What's the problem?

S: Our original plan is to arrange a direct vessel in the end of this month.

B: That's right.

S: We missed to book shipping space due to internal oversight, and there is no other direct vessel to your port this month. We need your agreement to allow transshipment, or we might

B：我是湯姆 史密斯。

S：您好！湯姆，我是倍斯特公司的湯尼 楊，我們對於貴司第1357號訂單的運輸安排恐怕出了點狀況。

B：是什麼問題呢？

S：我們原本預計在本月底安排直達船。

B：沒錯。

S：因內部疏失，我們錯過了訂艙，而這個月已經沒有直達船到達你方港口。請您允許轉船，否則我司將無法趕上您要求的到貨

208

not catch up on the required arrival date.

B: It should be feasible. But you're required to cover the extra transportation charge and the fee of L/C amendment to allow transshipment.

S: Naturally. Appreciate your assistance.

日。

B：這應該可行，但貴司須負擔額外的轉船費用及修改信用狀同意轉船的費用。

S：當然。感謝您的協助。

關鍵字彙

◎ **on hand** *ph.* 手頭上
　同義詞：available, at hand
　相關詞：on-hand balance 現有庫存量；adjust-on-hand 調整現有庫存量

◎ **express** *n.* [ɪkˋsprɛs] 快遞，快運
　同義詞：sending by speed
　相關詞：express consignment 快遞貨；express letter 快遞信件

◎ **favor** *n.* 恩惠，幫忙
　同義詞：kindness, benefit, good deed
　相關詞：do a favor 幫忙；in favor 贊同

◎ **partial** *a.* [ˋpɑrʃəl] 部分的，局部的
　同義詞：incomplete, uncomplete, part
　相關詞：partial adaptation 部分適應；partial blind 部分保密

freight collect *ph.* 運費到付

相關詞：freight prepaid 運費預付

解　析：運費到付是指出貨人不支付運付，而是由收貨人在目的地收到貨後支付運費。

allowance *n.* [əˋlaʊəns] 允許

同義詞：permission, permit, agreement

相關詞：make allowances for 考慮到

naturally *adv.* [ˋnætʃərəlɪ] 自然地，當然地

同義詞：certainly, surely, of course

相關詞：unnaturally；artificially 不自然地

catch up *ph.* 趕上

同義詞：bring up to date

相關詞：catch sight of 看到；catch a train 趕上火車

transport arrangement *ph.* 運輸安排

同義詞：shipment arrangement

相關詞：inland transport 內陸運輸；transportation reservation 運輸預定

direct vessel *ph.* 直達船

同義詞：direct boat, direct ship

相關詞：direct liner 直達班輪；direct steamer 直達汽船

book shipping space *ph.* 訂艙

同義詞：to charter space, to book cargo space

相關詞：book fee 訂艙費

關鍵句型

I need a big favor from you.......　　我需要你在某事物上的協助。

例句說明：

- **I need a big favor from you to** reply my inquiry by this weekend.
  我需要您協助在本週末前回覆我的詢價。

Is it possible to ...　　是否可能…

例句說明：

- **Is it possible to** reply to my inquiry by this weekend?
  是否有可能在本週末前回覆我的詢價？

have some difficulties in　　在…有困難

例句說明：

- We have some difficulties in accepting your counter offer.
  我們不太能接受您所提的還價。

We need your agreement to allow of Sth, or ...

我們需要你同意某事，否則…

例句說明：

- Mary **needs the** supervisor's **agreement to allow** one-day leave, or she'll miss the deadline of annual tax declaration.
  瑪莉需要主管准假一日，否則她會錯過年度報稅截止日。

Arrangement of Transshipment (required by seller)
安排轉船（賣方需求）

Dear Tom,

We're writing to inform you that we face some difficulties to arrange the shipment for your P/O No. 1357. We missed to book shipping space of the only direct vessel due to the carelessness and there is no other direct vessels to your port this month. Please grant us your acceptance of transshipment to make sure of the due delivery. In the meanwhile, the L/C should be amended to allow us the transshipment accordingly.

Please accept our apologies for any inconvenience we have caused. We will await your green signal to arrange the transshipment.

Sincerely yours,
Tony Yang

– 中文翻譯 –

湯姆 您好：

在此通知貴司我方對於貴司第1357號訂單的運輸安排出了點狀況。因疏忽，我司錯過了唯一一艘直達船的訂艙，而本月已沒有直達船到達你方港口。請允許我司轉船，以確保準時發貨。同時，請依此修改信用狀同意轉船。

若有不便，敬請見諒。將待貴司同意後安排轉船。

湯尼 楊 敬啟

Arrangement of Transshipment (Reply by Buyer)
分批裝運（買方回覆）

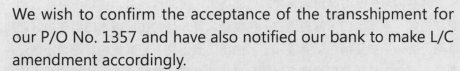

Dear Tony,

We wish to confirm the acceptance of the transshipment for our P/O No. 1357 and have also notified our bank to make L/C amendment accordingly.

Once receiving the notification of L/C amendment issued by the bank, please arrange the shipment at your earliest convenience.

Your prompt attention to this matter will be highly appreciated.

Sincerely yours,
Tom Smith

－ 中文翻譯 －

湯尼 您好：

我司在此確認接受第1357號訂單的轉船安排，並且已通知銀行依此修改信用狀。
待收到銀行改狀通知後，請盡一切可能馬上盡早安排裝船。
希望貴司對此事立即處理，我司將不勝感激。

湯姆 史密斯 敬啟

213

裝船指示

Shipping Instructions

國貿關鍵字 | 裝船指示 |

　　裝船指示是進口商載明貨物的裝運要求，通常包括公司資料、裝船日期、開船日期、起運港口、卸貨港口、包裝需求等，目的在於讓出口事先做好裝船準備。裝船通知又稱「裝運通知」。由出口商出具，記載貨物詳細裝運情況的通知，目的在於讓進口商做好接貨和付款的準備。裝船通知須依據買賣合約或信用狀規定的時間，由出口商發給進口商，無制式統一格式，唯以信用狀為付款條件時，裝船通知的內容一定要符合信用狀的規定。

情境說明

Buyer provides the seller the shipping instruction.

買方提供賣方裝船指示。

角色介紹

買方 | Buyer: B, ABC Co., Ltd.

賣方 | Seller: S, Best International Trade Corp.

情境對話

B: Good morning. Tom Smith speaking.

S: Good morning. Tom. This is Tony Yang calling from Best Corp. I'm just calling to let you know that your P/O No. 2468 will be ready for dispatch in two weeks.

B: Great to hear that.

B：早安，我是湯姆 史密斯。

S：早，湯姆，我是倍斯特公司的湯尼 楊。我打來是要通知您訂單號碼2468將於兩週後備妥出貨。

B：聽到這個消息太好了。

S: What I'd like to bring up for discussion is packing. Any special requirement about packing and shipping mark?

S：我想提出來討論的是包裝這事。關於包裝和運輸嘜頭，是否有特殊要求？

B: Yes. Please mark the cartons as per the drawing given to you this week.

B：是的。請依本週我司提供給您的圖樣來刷嘜。

S: Noted. Any additional requirement?

S：知道了。有其它額外需求嗎？

B: As the inner box is sales package, not transport package, the outer carton must be strong enough to withstand rough handling.

B：因內盒為銷售包裝，非運輸包裝，外箱須堅固到耐得住粗魯的搬運。

S: Please feel assured that we have especially reinforced our packing to minimize any possible damage to the goods.

S：請放心，我們已經特別加強包裝，以使貨物可能損壞的狀況減少到最低程度。

B: Could you use cardboard carton instead of carton to avoid damage caused in transit?

B：是否可以改用硬紙板箱，不用一般紙箱，以避免在運輸過程中損壞。

S: We can not afford the time for packing change at this moment.

S：現在我們來不及更換包裝了。

B: Well. I suppose there is no alternatives. I'll provide you the shipping instructions later.

B：好吧！看來別無選擇了，稍後我會給您裝船指示。

Buyer provides the seller with the shipping advice.

賣方提供裝船通知給買方。

角色介紹

買方 | Buyer: B, ABC Co., Ltd.

賣方 | Seller: S, Best International Trade Corp.

情境對話

S: Hello, Tom. This is Tony Yang calling from Best Corp.

S：您好！湯姆。我是倍斯特公司的湯尼 楊。

B: Hey, Tony. How's everything?

B：嘿！湯尼，你好啊！

S: I'm just calling to inform that the shipment against your P/O No. 2468 has been made via S.S "Ever Lembent" of Evergreen Marine.

S：我只為了要通知您貴司第2468號訂單已裝上長榮海運 "Ever Lembent" 號發貨。

B: It's great to hear that! What's the date of shipment?

B：喔！那太好了。出貨日是何時？

S: The vessel will be leaving H.K. on June 20. The estimated arrival date is July 20.

S：預計六月二十日由香港發船。預計七月二十日抵達倫敦。

B: Got it.

B：知道了。

S: The full set of shipping documents including cleaned on board B/L, Packing List, Certificate of Origin, Inspection Certification as well as Commercial Invoice will email to you tomorrow.

S：全套出貨文件包括清潔裝船提單、裝箱單、原產地證明書、檢驗報告及商業發票將於明天 email 給您。

B: Noted. I'll confirm once receiving the said shipping documents.

B：注意到了。當收到這些出貨文件時，我會跟您確認。

S: Just a kind reminder. We'll draw on you for the payment of L/C amounting to USD 20,000. Please protect the draft upon presentation.

S：提醒一下，我們會依信用狀金額20, 000美元開出匯票給您，在匯票提示時，請予以承兌。

B: Definitely. I will.

B：當然，我會的。

關鍵字彙

✓ **reinforce** *v.* [ˌriin`fɔrs] 增援，加強
同義詞：intensify, strengthen, increase

✓ **minimize** *v.* [`mɪnəˌmaɪz] 使減到最少，使縮到最小
同義詞：lessen, make small, reduce
相關詞：maximize 使增到最大

✓ **outer carton** *ph.* 外箱
相關詞：inner box, inner case 內盒

217

⊘ **withstand** *v.* [wɪð`stænd] 禁得起

同義詞：endure, resist, bear

相關詞：withstand high temperatures 耐高溫；withstand stresses 耐壓

⊘ **transport package** *ph.* 運輸包裝

相關詞：packaging materials 包裝材料

解　析：運輸包裝是為了降低運輸通過程中對產品造成損壞、保障產品安全及方便儲運裝卸。

⊘ **sales package** *ph.* 銷售包裝

相關詞：commodity packaging 商品包裝

解　析：銷售包裝又稱內包裝，是直接接觸商品並隨商品進入零售通路，為消費者直接可視的包裝。

⊘ **presentation** *n.* [ˌprɪzɛn`teʃən] 出示，提示，簡報

同義詞：present, presentment, demonstration

相關詞：presentation copy 贈送本

⊘ **include** *v.* [ɪn`klud] 包含

同義詞：consist of, involve, comprise

相關詞：not include; exclude 除外

⊘ **Packing List** *ph.* 裝箱單

相關詞：Packing Note

解　析：「裝箱單」是指記載商品包裝情況的單據，屬必要出貨文件之一，也是貨運單據中的一項重要單，Packing List 又稱 Packing Note 是貨物的包裝形式、包裝內容、數量、質量、體積或件數的單據。

⊘ **Certificate of Origin** *ph.* 產地證明書

相關詞：General Certificate of Origin 一般原產地證明書

解　析：「產地證明書」，又稱「原產地證明書」，簡稱 CO 是出口商應進口商要求而提供，由公證機構、政府或原廠出具，可證明貨物原產地或製造地的一種證明文件。

1

2

3 交貨條件 CHAPTER

4

關鍵句型

Please feel assured that ... 請放心⋯

例句說明：

· **Please feel assured that** we will release the shipment on time.
請放心我們一定準時出貨。

draw on Sb. for ... 為⋯向某人開出匯票/支票

例句說明：

· I'm the bearer of check **drawn on you for** the payment of USD500.
我持有一張由你兌付500美元款項的支票。

職場經驗談

易混淆的船運相關文件比一比：

1. 裝船指示（**Shipping Instruction**）：是進口商在貨物備妥之前發給出口商，載明貨物的裝運說明，通常包括船公司資料、裝船日期、開船日期、起運港口、卸貨港口、包裝需求等，其目的在於讓出口商有足夠的時間做好裝船準備。

2. 裝船通知（**Shipping Advice**）：由出口商在貨物備妥裝船後發給進口商，通知貨物已裝船的通知單，內容通常包括貨物詳細裝運情況，目的在於讓進口商做好付款和接貨的準備。

3. 出口貨物明細單（**Shipping Bill**）：又稱「貨物出運分析單」，是指託運人依據買賣合約條款和信用狀條款內容所填寫，藉以向運輸公司或貨運代理公司申辦貨物托運的單證。

4. 裝貨單（**Shipping Order**，簡稱**S/O**）：又稱「關單」，是指承運人(船公司)在接受託運人提出托運申請後，發給託運人的單證，同時也是船長將貨物裝船的憑證。通常只有經海關簽章後的裝貨單，船方才能收貨裝船。

Shipping Instruction 裝船指示

Dear Tony,

We are delighted to inform you that we have opened an irrevocable sight L/C No.125 with amount of USD20,000 in your favor. Please arrange the shipment as soon as you receive it.

We'd like to call your attention that each part should be wrapped with double cotton papers to avoid damage during transportation and packed in cardboard carton. Besides, the shipping mark should be as below:

ABC

P/O No. 2468
Nos. 3-20
London via H.K.
20 x 10 x 8 FT.
G.W. 500 KGS
Made In Taiwan
We'll await your shipping advice in soon.

Sincerely yours,
Tom Smith

– 中文翻譯 –

湯尼 您好：

很高興通知貴司，我方已開立給您不可撤銷即期信用狀第 125 號，金額為20,000美元。請收到後立即安排船運。

請注意單一產品需使用雙層棉紙包裝，避免在運輸過程中受損，並請使用硬紙箱包裝。此外，請依下列所示刷嘜：

ABC

P/O No. 2468

Nos. 3-20

London via H.K.

20 x 10 x 8 FT.

G.W. 500 KGS

Made In Taiwan

期待儘早收到貴司的裝船通知。

湯姆 史密斯 敬啟

短收通知與漏裝處理

Notification of short delivery and make-up for short delivery

國貿關鍵字 │ 漏裝與短收 │

漏裝是指貨物已經進出口港並完成報關，但在裝船時因故不能上船，則需由船公司安排裝載至另一艘船貨延至下一航次，一般而言出口商不需再次報關。倘若海關不同意以(漏裝)為之，出口商則不得不辦理退關手續，待重新訂艙，並取得提單號碼後，再次做報關申報。

情境說明

Buyer notifies sellers about the short delivery.
買方通知賣方貨物短收。

角色介紹
買方│Buyer: B, ABC Co., Ltd.
賣方│Seller: S, Best International Trade Corp.

情境對話

B: Hello. This is Tom Smith from ABC Co.

B：您好！我是ABC公司的湯姆 史密斯。

S: Hey, Tom. What can I do for you today?

S：嘿！湯姆，今天有什麼能為您效勞的地方嗎？

B: Listen. The goods against our P/O No. 2468 shipped via S.S "Ever

S：第2468號訂單已於這星期由長榮海運Ever Lembent

Lembent" of Evergreen Marine had reached our port this Monday, but we can't locate carton No. 20.

號運抵我方港口，但我們沒看到二十號箱。

S: It is remotely possible.

S：這不太可能。

B: We are wondering if the shortage was due to the carelessness by your side or the carrier.

B：不知是否因為貴司或運送人的疏忽導致短少。

S: We were sure that the whole batch with total 30 cartons was loaded on board. That was proved by clean onboard B/L.

S：我們確認有安排整批貨共三十箱裝船，清潔裝船提單可為佐證。

B: Anyway, as we are in urgent need of the lost parts. Please conduct an investigation in to this matter as soon as possible.

B：無論如何，因為我司急需此批遺失的貨，請儘速進行調查。

S: Naturally. We will carry out the inquiry expeditiously and let you know the result as soon as we can.

S：當然，我們將儘快進行調查，並儘速讓您知道結果。

The shipping company makes up to the seller for the short delivery.

船公司處理賣方的漏裝貨物。

情境對話

C: Evergreen Marine Corp., this is David speaking.

C：這裡是長榮海運，我是大衛。

S: Hello, David. This is Tony Yang from Best Co. I'm calling to track the investigation progress about the short delivery of the goods shipped via S.S "Ever Lembent."

S：您好！大衛。我是倍斯特公司的湯尼 楊。我打來追蹤關於 "Ever Lembent" 號短出貨的調查進度。

C: Yes, Mr. Yang. Regarding your last phone claiming for the short quantity loaded against B/L No. 123, we have found the missing carton in the port of loading.

C：是的，楊先生，關於上次電話中要求索賠提單號碼123的漏裝事宜，我們已在裝船港找到遺失的箱子。

S: I am glad of hearing that. What was this mistake caused by?

S：真高興聽到這個訊息！是哪裡出錯呢？

C: This error was largely due to the

C：這個錯誤主要是由於運送

224

oversight by the carrier. We'll arrange the cargo delivery to the original destination you assigned.

人疏忽造成。我們將安排產品運送至您指定的原目的港。

S: Please ensure to give me a notification once the delivery takes place.

S：待出貨時請務必通知我。

C: We will, for sure. Please accept our deep apologies for any inconvenience it may cause to you and your customers.

C：會的，這是當然的。對於造成貴司及貴司客戶任何不便，希望您見諒。

關鍵字彙

✓ **remotely** *adv.* [rɪ`motlɪ] 遙遠地，極少地
同義詞：far way, distantly, in a remote way
相關詞：remote manipulation 遠距操作

✓ **carrier** *n.* [`kærɪɚ] 運送人，搬運人
同義詞：transporter, messenger, bringer
相關詞：letter carrier 郵差；carrier bag 購物袋

✓ **inquiry** *n.* [ɪn`kwaɪrɪ] 詢問，調查
同義詞：search for information, inquiry, query
相關詞：inquiry data 調查數據；inquiry office 詢問處

✓ **expeditiously** *adv.* [ˌɛkspɪ`dɪʃəslɪ] 迅速地
同義詞：swiftly, efficiently, quickly
相關詞：carefully and expeditiously 仔細且快速

⊘ **carton No.** *ph.* 箱號

相關詞：shipping mark 運輸標誌

解　析：運輸標誌，又稱嘜頭，由一個簡單的幾何圖形和一些字母、數字及簡單的文字組成，其作用在於使貨物在裝卸、運輸、保管過程中易於辨識，避免裝運錯誤。主要可分為正嘜和側嘜，而側嘜則包含「箱號」等其它運輸所需內容，如許可證號、品號、訂單號碼、產品毛淨重、體積、裝箱等。側嘜範例如下：

ITEM NO: CH6688

PCS/CTN: 20PCS / No. 4

N.W.: 800 KGS

G.W.: 750 KGS

MEAS:

⊘ **track** *v.* [træk] 追蹤，追查

同義詞：investigate, follow

相關詞：track point 跟蹤點；track down 查獲

⊘ **short delivery** *ph.* 短出

同義詞：short shipment

相關詞：over shipment 溢出

⊘ **port of loading** *ph.* 裝運港

同義詞：Port of Shipment 裝運港

解　析：裝運港是指將貨物裝上運輸工具的港口。

⊘ **assign** *v.* [əˋsaɪn] 指定

同義詞：appoint, name

相關詞：assign to a job 指派工作；assigned store 指定商店

⊘ **notification** *n.* [ˌnotəfəˋkeʃən] 通知

同義詞：notice

相關詞：release the notification 發出通知；email notification 電郵通知

✅ **take place** *ph.* 發生

同義詞：happen, occur, come about

相關詞：meetings to take place weekly 開週會

關鍵句型

We are sure that ... 我們非常確認 …

例句說明：

· **We are sure that** we will both profit from the trade with each other.

我們非常確認雙方會在此筆交易中獲利。

Sth. be proved by ... 某事經由…獲得證實

例句說明：

· Your good performance **is proved by** the promotion.

你的良好表現已由此次晉升獲得證實。

Regarding your last phone claiming for ...

有關於上次電話談話中要求索賠 …

例句說明：

· **Regarding your last phone claiming for** defective parts, we'll deliver the qualified parts as soonas we can.

有關於上次電話談話中要求索賠瑕疵品，我們會盡速寄出合格品。

This error is largely due to ... 此錯誤主要起因於…

例句說明：

· **This error is largely due to** his inexperience in business.

此錯誤主要起因於他在商業上經驗不足。

英文書信這樣寫

Notification of Short Delivery 短收通知

Dear Tony,

Please be informed that the goods against our P/O No. 2468 shipped via S.S "Ever Lembent" of Evergreen Marine had arrived at our end last Monday.

Unfortunately, we can't locate carton No. 20 and are wondering if the shortage was due to the carelessness on your side or the carrier.

Please notify the shipping company of the loss and keep us posted of the investigation result once available.

Sincerely yours,
Tom Smith

- 中文翻譯 -

湯尼 您好：

在此通知貴司，第2468號訂單已於本週一由長榮海運"Ever Lembent"號運抵我方。

很不幸的是我們沒收到第二十號箱，懷疑是否因為貴司或運送人的疏忽導致短少。

請盡快通知船公司此短缺事宜，請獲得調查結果後，馬上通知我司知悉。

湯姆 史密斯 敬啟

Make-up for Short Delivery 漏裝處理

Dear Sirs,

We just received the notification from our client that only 29 cartons out of 30 cartons, shipped via S.S "Ever Lembent" on June 10, had been delivered. The carton No. 20 couldn't be located in the container.

We suspect that the shortage could only have happened in transit and the responsibility for the shortage should rest with you. In this case, please go on with the investigation and we reserve the right to make a claim with you for the loss.

Sincerely yours,
Tony Yang

－ 中文翻譯 －

敬啟者：

我司客戶通知由 "Ever Lembent" 號承運的三十箱貨，僅二十九箱抵達，第二十號箱並未在貨櫃內。

我司懷疑短缺是發生在運途中，而責任會歸屬於貴司。因此，請對此事進行調查，而我方將保留向貴司索賠損失的權利。

湯尼 楊 敬啟

交貨延遲和數量不符

Delayed Shipment and Error Shipping Quantity

國貿關鍵字 | 交貨延遲的補救 |

　　一般來說交貨延遲的原因大多是因為不可抗力(Force Majeure)，是指在合約簽訂後，非因契約雙方當事人任何一方之過失或疏忽，而是發生了當事人無法預見且無法事先防範的意外事故，以致於無法履行合約或不能如期履行合約。在此情況下，遭受意外事故的一方可以免除履行合約的責任或延期履行合約。可以分為兩種情況：自然災害如水災、火災或暴風雪和社會因素如戰爭、罷工、抗爭和政府禁令。

情境說明

Buyer complains about delayed shipment by the seller.

買方抱怨賣方交貨延遲。

角色介紹

買方 | Buyer: B, ABC Co., Ltd.

賣方 | Seller: S, Best International Trade Corp.

情境對話

S: Hello, Tony. This is Tom Smith from Best International Trade Corp. I want to inform you about the goods against your P/O No. 8888.

S：您好，湯尼，我是倍斯特公司的湯姆 史密斯。我想告知您有關你的第8888號訂單的這批貨。

B: Hi, Tom, How are you?

B：哈囉，湯姆，你好嗎？

S: It will be late for two week and two weeks later than the original ETA. Please accept our deep apologies for the delay.

S：這批貨會晚到且比原定到貨日晚兩周才抵達。很抱歉運送延遲。

B: What is the reason causing the delivery delay?

B：是什麼原因造成運送延遲呢？

S: It was mainly due to the bad weather during the transit.

S：主要是運途中氣候惡劣所致。

B: The late delivery will lead to the serious short supply to our customer.

B：這次的運送延遲會導致我司客戶嚴重供貨不足。

S: We're sincerely sorry to hear this news. Please kindly understand that the force majeure as weather condition is out of our control. If the situation improves, we will definitely keep posting with further updates.

S：我們真的對這個消息感到很抱歉，但是請諒解氣候狀況屬不可抗力事件，我們也無力可防範。我們會隨時向您報告最新的運送消息。

Buyer complains to seller about error shipping quantity.

買方向賣方抱怨交貨數量不正確。

買方｜Buyer: B, ABC Co., Ltd.

賣方｜Seller: S, Best International Trade Corp.

情境對話

B: Hello, Tony. This is Tom Smith from ABC Co.

B：您好，湯尼，我是ABC公司的湯姆 史密斯。

S: Hello, Tom. How is the goods against your P/O No. 8888?

S：您好，湯姆。貴司第8888號訂單的這批貨如何呢？

B: That's exactly why I am calling. We found that the carton didn't contain the required quantity we ordered.

B：這正是我打來給您的原因。我們發現箱子內裝的數量不符合我們的訂購量。

S: We apologize for sendind the insufficient quantity due to the carelessness of our worker.

S：很抱歉因為我們的疏失導致出貨數量不足。

B: Please deliver the remaining parts to us as soon as you can at freight prepaid.

B：請儘速以運費預付的方式安排寄出剩餘的數量。

S: Definitely. We'll deal with it at once.

S：當然。我會立即處理此事。

B: We will not <u>require compensation for</u> our loss caused by the mistake but please promise it will never happen again.

S: Appreciate your kindness. We'll take corrective actions to ensure such mistake will not occur in the future.

B：我司將不會針對此次運送錯誤所造成的損失提出賠償。但請保證不再發生。

S：感謝您的善意。我司保證會採取改善措施，確保未來不再發生此類錯誤。

關鍵字彙

✓ **mainly** *adv.* [ˋmanly] 主要地
同義詞：chiefly, principally, primarily
相關詞：A be mainly made up of B　A主要由B組成

✓ **transit** *n.* [ˋtrænsɪt] 運輸，運送
同義詞：transportation, transition, passage
相關詞：transit the merchandises 貨物轉口；transit box 轉運箱

✓ **force majeure** *ph.* 不可抗力（如天災、戰爭等）
同義詞：act of God, vis major, inevitable accident
相關詞：force-majeure clause 不可抗力條款

✓ **short supply** *ph.* 供貨不足
同義詞：insufficient supply
相關詞：supply-demand balance 供需平衡

✓ **out of control** *ph.* 不受控制
同義詞：not in control, out of hand
相關詞：in the control of 控制中；lose control of 失去控制

⊘ **carelessness** *n.* [ˋkɛrlɪsnɪs] 粗心大意

同義詞：negligence, incaution, lack of caution

相關詞：carefulness 細心

⊘ **remaining** *a.* [rɪˋmenɪŋ] 剩下的

同義詞：extra, surplus, excess

相關詞：remaining amount 餘額；remaining time 剩餘時間

⊘ **occur** *v.* [əˋkɝ] 發生

同義詞：happen, come about, take place

相關詞：occur to 想到；occurrence 事件，發生

⊘ **make compensation** *ph.* 賠償

同義詞：compensate, pay back

相關詞：legal compensation 法定賠償

⊘ **corrective action** *ph.* 改下措施

同義詞：corrective measure 校正措施

相關詞：corrective control 校正控制；corrective element 校正要素

關鍵句型

I have to complain about ...　我必須抱怨⋯

例句說明：

> · **I have to complain about** your late reply.
> 我必須抱怨您延遲回覆我。

What is the reason causing ...　造成⋯的原因為何？

例句說明：

> · **What is the reason causing** your late reply?
> 造成你延遲回覆的原因為何？

We found that ...　我們發現⋯

例句說明：

> · **We found that** your offer is much higher than competitors'.
> 我們發現貴司的報價比同業高出許多。

We will not make compensation for ...　我們將不會賠償⋯

例句說明：

> · **We will not make compensation for** the damaged package.
> 我們將不會對包裝損毀賠償。

英文書信這樣寫

Delay Shipment (Complaint from Buyer)
交貨延遲（買方抱怨）

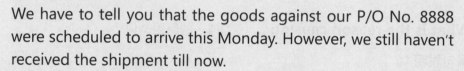

Dear Tony,

We have to tell you that the goods against our P/O No. 8888 were scheduled to arrive this Monday. However, we still haven't received the shipment till now.

We hope that you can find out the reason for the delay problern as soon as possible. Just a kind reminder that the delivery postponement for more than one week will break the terms of the contract.

Your prompt attention to this matter will be appreciated.

Sincerely yours,
Tom Smith

— 中文翻譯 —

湯尼 您好：

我司必須告知貴司，我司第8888號訂單的產品應於本週一到達，但截至目前我司仍未收到貨物。

我司希望貴司能儘快查明運送延遲的原因。提醒貴司，若此批貨延期超過一週，將違反合約條款。

若您能對此事立即處理，我司將不勝感激。

湯姆 史密斯 敬啟

Delay Shipment (Reply from Seller)
交貨延遲（賣方回覆）

Dear Tom,

Please accept our sincere apologies for the shipment postponement for your P/O No. 8888.

Kindly be advised that the delay was mainly caused by a severe typhoon during the delivery. The ship is expected to arrive at the destination 3 days later than scheduled.

We hope you can understand the situation this time.

Sincerely yours,
Tony Yang

－ 中文翻譯 －

湯姆 您好：

很抱歉對於您第8888號訂單運送延遲。

在此貴司此次延遲是因運輸過程中遇強烈颱風所造成，貨物將比預計時間晚三天到達。

希望您能諒解我司此情況。

湯尼 楊 敬啟

外觀損壞和功能瑕疵

Cosmetic and Functional Defects

國貿關鍵字 | 發現損壞或瑕疵問題 |

　　貨物在進出口時，難免在運送途中會有損壞或是收到貨品後才發現瑕疵問題，有些廠商會在某一限額內多出貨或是再次出貨，但因考量到再次運輸時間，一發現問題必須馬上與進口商聯絡並尋求解決方案，以免嚴重影響後續生產進度。

情境說明

Buyer complains to the seller about cosmetic defects of products.

買方抱怨賣方產品外觀損壞。

角色介紹

買方 | Buyer: B, ABC Co., Ltd.

賣方 | Seller: S, Best International Trade Corp.

情境對話

B: Hello, Tony. This is Tom Smith from ABC Co.

S: Hello, Tom. How is the goods against your P/O No. 8888?

B: That's exactly why I am calling. We found that some parts are with

B：您好，湯尼，我是ABC公司的湯姆 史密斯。

S：您好，湯姆。貴司第8888號訂單的這批貨如何呢？

B：這正是我打電話給您的原因。開箱時我們發現部分

cosmetic defect caused by improper handling when we opened the carton.

產品因處理不當造成外觀不良。

S: I really regret to hear this bad news. What's the defect rate?

S：很抱歉聽到這個壞消息，不良比例為何？

B: Nearly 25% of the parts are defective. What shall we do with the defective pats? Should we return to you or scrap locally?

B：有將近25%的不良品。我們應如何處置不良品呢？退回給您或當地報廢？

S: Is it possible that you accept the defective parts, and then we will charge you at half price?

S：您是否有可能接受這些不良品，而我司可僅收半價？

B: I can't make the decision at this moment without consulting our engineer. I'll have to confirm if there's any functionality concern.

B：我得先問一下我司工程師意見，我現在無法做決定，必須進一步與工程師確認此不良是否有功能上的疑慮。

S: That's fine. Please get back to me once available.

S：好啊！請在知道結果後通知我。

情境說明

Buyer complains to seller about function defects of products.

買方抱怨賣方的產品功能瑕疵。

買方 | Buyer: B, ABC Co., Ltd.

賣方 | Seller: S, Best International Trade Corp.

情境對話

B: Hello, Tony. This is Tom Smith from ABC Co.

B：你好，湯尼，我是ABC公司的湯姆 史密斯。

S: Hello, Tom. How is the goods against your P/O No. 8888?

S：你好，湯姆。貴司第8888號訂單的這批貨如何？

B: That's exactly why I am calling. We found an assembly problem with your products.

B：這正是我打給您的原因。我們發現貴司的產品有組裝上的問題。

S: That surprises me! Could you describe the problem?

S：我太驚訝了。你能描述問題嗎？

B: The part can't fit properly with its mating part. We need your advice on this problem.

B：產品不能與它的零件實配。我們需要你對此問題給建議。

S: Before we recall lots, please return us several pieces of the defective parts

S：在我們召回該批貨之前，請退回幾件有缺陷產品連

along with its mating parts to identify the defect.

B: OK, I'll arrange the delivery of the required parts immediately. As we're in dire need of the parts, please deal with this issue as soon as you can.

S: Once confirming the liability is certainly on our side, we will send the new parts for replacement at once.

同配件，讓我們找出不良原因。

B：好的，我會立即安排寄出所需的產品。我們急需要此產品，請儘早處理這個問題。

S：一旦確認責任在我方，我們將立即寄出替換的新產品做更換。

關鍵字彙

⊘ **cosmetic** *a.* [kɑz`mɛtɪk] 裝飾性的；表面的
同義詞：ornamental, decorative, nonfunctional
相關詞：cosmetic surface 外觀面，裝飾面

⊘ **nearly** *adv.* [`nɪrlɪ] 幾乎，差不多
同義詞：almost, closely, all but
相關詞：nearly empty 幾乎空了；nearly ready 快備妥了

⊘ **functionality** *n.* [ˌfʌnkʃə`nælɪtɪ] 功能
同義詞：usefulness
相關詞：functionality issues 功能議題；extra functionality 額外功能

⊘ **improper handling** *ph.* 處理不當
同義詞：mishandling，mismanagement
相關詞：handling cost 處理費

⊘ **the defect rate** *ph.* 不良比例

同義詞：percentage of non-conforming quality

相關詞：defect mark 瑕疵點；defective packing 包裝不良

⊘ **scrap locally** *ph.* 當地報廢

同義詞：write off topically dispose locally

相關詞：scrap value 殘值

⊘ **describe** *v.* [dɪ`skraɪb] 描寫，敘述

同義詞：define, characterize, portray, delineate

相關詞：describe oneself

⊘ **fit** *v.* [fɪt] 組配

同義詞：match, equal, mate

相關詞：fit for, suitable for 適合；fit in 裝配好

⊘ **advice** *n.* [əd`vaɪs] 勸告，忠告

同義詞：suggestion, counsel, guidance

相關詞：advice of drawing 匯票/支票通知

⊘ **recall** *v.* [rɪ`kɔl] 回想，回憶，召回

同義詞：remember, recollect, think back

相關詞：cars recall 汽車召回；product recall 產品召回

⊘ **liability** *n.* [ˌlaɪə`bɪlətɪ] 責任，義務

同義詞：responsibility, obligation

相關詞：liability insurance 責任保險

⊘ **in dire need** *ph.* 太需要

同義詞：in such a need，in desperate need

相關詞：less need 不太需要

關鍵句型

What shall we do with ... 我們應該如何做⋯

例句說明：

· **What shall we do with** the production residues?
我們應該如何處理生產多餘產品。

I can't make the decision without ... 沒有⋯，我無法做決定。

例句說明：

· **I can't make the decision without** consulting my lawyer.
沒有諮詢律師前，我無法做決定。

We need your advice about/on Sth.
我們需要你對某事的建議。

例句說明：

· **We need your advice** solving financial problem.
我們需要你對解決財務問題的建議。

Cosmetic Defect (Notification from Buyer)
外觀損壞（買方通知）

Dear Tony,

I regret to inform you that nearly 25% of the goods against our P/O. 8888 delivered to us was received with handling damage as shown on the attached photos. I'll send the defective parts back to you for exchange.

Please let us know the process regarding to receiving replacement and confirm with us upon receipt of our returned part.

Sincerely yours,
Tom Smith

─ 中文翻譯 ─

湯尼 您好：

很遺憾通知貴司，您寄給我司第8888號訂單的產品有將近25%有的損傷，照片如附件。我將寄還損壞的產品回貴司，以利換。

請告知我司有關替換貨的流程，待貴司收到退還貨物後，亦請通知我司一聲。

湯姆 史密斯 敬啟

Cosmetic Defect (Reply from Buyer)
外觀損壞（賣方回覆）

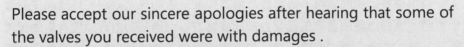

Dear Tom,

Please accept our sincere apologies after hearing that some of the valves you received were with damages .

We thought that the problem should have occurred due to improper delivery and will negotiate with the shipping company right away. Meanwhile, we will send replacements to you shortly for.

Sorry again for the trouble caused to you.

Sincerely yours,
Tony Yang

– 中文翻譯 –

湯姆您好：
很抱歉貴司收到的產品發生有部分處理不當造成之損傷。

我司認為應為運送不當所致，我們會立即與運輸公司協商。同時，我司亦會馬上寄出新產品給貴司進行更換。

造成您的困擾，再次致歉。

湯尼 楊 敬啟

客訴－包裝損毀和回覆延遲
Complaint - Package Damage and Late Response

國貿關鍵字 │ 延遲的回覆 │

發現貨物出現問題時，或當賣方無法如期於合約規定期限完成產品生產及出貨時，實務上應由賣方主動發通知知會買方，而通知的內容須包含貨物延遲原因、新的交貨日期或期限、無法如期履行交貨承諾時的相關配套促施，如買方有權決定部份出貨或訂單全數取消，和無法履行交貨承諾的賠償等。

情境說明

Buyer complains to the seller about packaging damage.

買方抱怨賣方公司的產品包裝損毀。

角色介紹

買方 │ Buyer: B, ABC Co., Ltd.

賣方 │ Seller: S, Best International Trade Corp.

情境對話

B: Hello, Tony. This is Tom Smith from ABC Co.

B：你好，湯尼。我是ABC公司的湯姆 史密斯。

S: Hello, Tom. How is the goods against your P/O No. 8888?

S：你好，湯姆。貴司第8888號訂單的這批貨如何呢？

B: We have received the lots yesterday but found most of the cartons are in

B：我們已在昨天收到這批貨，但發現大部分的紙箱

bad condition.

S: We are sorry to hear of a great deal of breakage, which might be caused by weak cartons. What's the part condition?

B: After making a complete inspection, all the goods are <u>in good condition except</u> one carton with severe damaged parts which can't be used. <u>We'll send you the pictures showing</u> the defects of both the cartons and parts.

S: We will exchange the damaged parts by freight prepaid at once.

B: Great. How shall we deal with the defective parts?

S: Please scrap the parts locally and offer us the scrap value.

損壞。

B：我們很抱歉聽到紙箱大量破損的消息，可能導因於不堅固的紙箱。產品的情況如何？

S：經過完全檢查之後，確認所有的貨物都完好無損，除了一個紙箱內產品損壞嚴重不能使用。我們會提供顯示紙箱和零件缺陷的照片給貴司。

B：我們將透過運費預付，立即更換有損壞的紙箱和貨物。

S：太好了，我們應如何處理這些不良品？

B：請就在當地報廢，並提供給我們報廢殘值。

情境說明

Buyer complains they haven't got any email reply from the seller.

買方抱怨遲遲未收到賣方公司的email回覆。

角色介紹

買方｜Buyer: B, ABC Co., Ltd.

賣方｜Seller: S, Best International Trade Corp.

情境對話

B: Hello, Tony. This is Tom Smith from ABC Co.

B：您好！湯尼，我是ABC公司的湯姆 史密斯。

S: Hello, Tom. What can I do for you?

S：您好！湯姆，有什麼能為您效勞的地方？

B: We were notified that the shipment of our P/O No. 4455 will be delayed. I sent several e-mails to you, but we haven't got any news about specific production schedule and no updated shipping schedule up to now.

B：我們接獲通知第4455號訂單的出貨將延期。我寄了幾封 email 給您，但截至目前都還未得到具體生產進度及更新交期。

S: I've been tied up with the trade show these days, so I have had little time to check my emails box. Please accept my sincere apology.

S：我這幾天忙於貿易展，因此沒有太多時間查看 email 信箱。還請見諒。

B: Never mind. Please make sure to

B：沒關係。下次請即時回覆我的信件。

respond to my email with punctuality next time.

S: Definitely, I will. <u>Please send your email to</u> my secretary next time, who will remind me to deal with the urgent case at once.

S：我絕對會的。下次請將副本寄給我的秘書，他會提醒我立即處理緊急事件。

關鍵字彙

☑ **a great deal of** *ph.* 大量的，許多的

同義詞：a good deal of, a great amount of, a huge deal of

相關詞：a great deal of cost 大量的成本；a great deal of differences 相差甚遠

☑ **breakage** *n.* [`brekɪdʒ] 破損，毀壞

同義詞：fracture, act of breaking

相關詞：a great deal of breakage 損壞許多

☑ **weak** *a.* [wik] 脆弱的

同義詞：frail, poor

相關詞：weak-headed 易碎的；weak market 市場疲軟

☑ **in bad condition** *ph.* 裝況不佳

同義詞：in poor condition, in poor shape

相關詞：in bad taste 粗俗

☑ **prepaid** *a.* [pri`ped] 預付的

同義詞：paid in advance

相關詞：prepayment 預付款

⊘ **scrap value** *ph.* 報廢殘值

同義詞：value as leftovers, value for junk material

相關詞：scrap yard 報廢場；scrap-heap 廢料堆

⊘ **schedule** *n.* [ˋskɛdʒʊl] 時間表

同義詞：timeable, plan

相關詞：on schedule 準時；ahead of schedule 提前, 提早

⊘ **respond** *v.* [rɪˋspɑnd] 回答

同義詞：answer, reply

相關詞：respon (n.) 回答；respondency (n.) 回應；respondent (n.) 應答者

⊘ **punctuality** *n.* [͵pʌŋktʃʊˋælətɪ] 準時

同義詞：being on time

相關詞：unpunctuality；lack of punctuality 不準時

⊘ **production schedule** *ph.* 生產計畫

同義詞：manufacturing schedule

相關詞：production progress 生產進度；production cost 生產成本

⊘ **up to now** *ph.* 到目前為止

同義詞：till now, as yet, to date

⊘ **deal with** *ph.* 處理

同義詞：handle, take care of, treat

相關詞：close a deal with 成交

關鍵句型

Sth. be in good condition except ... 　某物狀況佳，除了…之外。

例句說明：

· The operation system **is in good condition except** the software which is out-of-date.

除了軟體未更新之外，作業系統狀況良好。

We'll send you the picture showing ... 　我們會提供你…的照片。

例句說明：

· **We'll send you the picture showing** the loaded container before delivery.

出貨前我們會提供裝櫃的照片給你。

I've been tied up with ... 　我忙於…

例句說明：

· **I've been tied up with** the production planning.

我忙於安排生產排程。

copy your email to Sb. 　將電郵副本寄給某人

例句說明：

· Please must **copy your email to** my supervisor as well.

請務必也將 email 寄給我的上司。

Delayed Response (Complaint from Buyer)
回覆延遲（買方抱怨）

Dear Tony,

I'm writing to check production schedule of our open orders.

Several emails were sent to you for getting the updated status, but there has been no response from your end so far. That leaves us feeling very disappointed.

We urgently request a reasonable explanation from you about this issue.

Sincerely yours,
Tom Smith

─ 中文翻譯 ─

湯尼 您好：

這封信是想詢問我司訂單的生產計劃。

我司已多次發信詢問最新情況，但截至目前為止仍未收到您的回覆，此情況令我們備感失望。

針對此事，請您儘快提出合理說明。

湯姆 史密斯 敬啟

知識補給

　　生產計劃（**Production Schedule**）是指為同時滿足客戶對訂單的三大訴求「交期、品質、成本」，以及確保企業能獲得適當利益，而對生產的三大訴求「材料、人員、機器設備」所做的計畫，以確切準備、分配及運用資源。

執行生產計劃的最終目的在於：
1. 確保交貨日期
2. 穩定生產量，避免產能過剩或產能吃緊
3. 控制庫存水平
4. 原物料採購的參考依據
5. 現場員工調度或職工招聘的參考依據
6. 擴充生產設備的參考依據

生產計劃的內容一般包含如下：
1. 產品名稱及零件名稱
2. 生產的數量或重量
3. 生產部門及單位（依個別產品生產工序不同而定）
4. 起始日
5. 生產需求完成日及交期

Chapter 4

買賣、運輸、保險賠償

Claim with seller, shipping company and insurance company

人為損壞和自然災害索賠

Claim for shipping damage with shipping company and natural disaster with insurance company

國貿關鍵字 | 運輸索賠 |

運輸索賠(Transportation Claim)是指貨物在裝卸及運輸過程中，因承運人的原因所導致的損失，進口商可直接向承運人、其代理人和保險公司提出損害賠償。

情境說明

Buyer requests buyer to make a claim for shipping damage with the shipping company.

賣方要求買方向運輸公司提出運輸損壞索賠。

角色介紹

買方 | Buyer: B, ABC Co., Ltd.

賣方 | Seller: S, Best International Trade Corp.

情境對話

B: Hi, Tony. This is Tom Smith at ABC Co.

B：您好！湯尼，我是ABC 公司的湯姆 史密斯

S: How are things, Tom?

S：最近如何，湯姆？

B: Just fine. Sorry to let you know that we have a claim to make against you for the 2,000pcs ball valves of our P/O No. 3366 we just received. We

B：一切都好。很抱歉通知您我們有一項索賠申請，是針對我們剛收到的第3366號訂單中的2,000件球閥。

found nearly 50% of parts were broken.

我們發現近50%的產品破損。

S: Yeah, I <u>acknowledged</u> the receipt of the survey's report and the photo sent by your QA engineer and just finished the review.

S：是的，我確認收到了貴司品保工程師提供的調查報告和照片也剛看完。

B: The parts are too much damaged to be used, which and impact available supplies. We need you to arrange a product exchange by air freight at your cost immediately.

B：產品損壞太嚴重無法使用，這會影響我們供貨。我們需要您以空運運費預付的方式立即安排換貨。

S: The lots were packed as per your packing instructions without change. As you can see from the photo, the packing was almost in good order.

S：此批貨是依據您的包裝指示包裝的，未做更動，從照片可以看出，包裝幾乎是完好無缺。

B: Hmm, I'm not really sure about your statement.

B：嗯，我不能太肯定。

S: I am quite sure that such damage could have happened in transit due to rough handling. The claim concerning transportation should be referred to the carrier or shipping company.

S：我相當肯定此品質問題可能是在運輸途中搬運不當所致，涉及運輸問題的索賠應向承運人或船公司提出。

B: <u>Provided that is true</u>, we'll do so.

B：倘若真的如此，我們會這樣做。

257

角色介紹
買方│Buyer: B, ABC
Co., Ltd.
賣方│Seller: S, Best
International Trade
Corp.

情境說明

Seller notifies buyer that a claim for natural disaster will be made with insurance company.

賣方通知買方，其將向保險公司提出天然災害索賠。

情境對話

S: This is Tony Yang. What can I do for you?

S：我是湯尼 楊，有什麼能為您效勞的？

B: Hello, Tony. It's Tom Smith from ABC Co. I have got a bad news with the goods against our P/O No. 2233 for you.

B：你好，湯尼，我是ABC 公司的湯姆 史密斯，有一個關於我們第2233號訂單的壞消息要告訴您。

S: What's wrong?

S：有什麼問題呢？

B: Owing to the inclement weather, the container containing our goods was washed away overboard by a huge wave.

B：因天氣惡劣，巨浪把裝載此批貨的貨櫃從船上捲落海裡了。

S: That's too terrible.

S：那真是太糟糕了。

B: As the above loss is under the coverage granted by insurance

B：上述損失在保險公司的承保範圍，我們會向該保險

company, we'll lodge the claim with the insurance company.

公司提出索賠。

S: I see. If there's Anything I can do for you, please let me know.

S：了解。如果有什麼能為您做的，再請告訴我。

B: Well. I do need your favor to arrange immediate production run for the missing lots. Otherwise, we'll face the situation of insufficient stock.

B：好吧。我確實需要您幫忙對此批遺失的貨物安排立即投產。否則，我們就會面臨存貨不足的情況。

S: OK. Let me check our production plan and provide the feedback to you later.

S：好吧。讓我檢查一下我們的生產規劃，稍後回覆您。

關鍵字彙

⊘ **acknowledge** *v.* [əkˋnɑlɪdʒ] 告知收到
同義詞：certify the receipt of
相關詞：refuse to acknowledge 不理

⊘ **exchange** *v.* [ɪksˋtʃendʒ] 交換
同義詞：change, interchange, switch
相關詞：foreign exchange 外匯；exchange rate 匯率

⊘ **statement** *n.* [ˋstetmənt] 陳述，說明
同義詞：report, announcement, proclamation
相關詞：to issue a statement 發表；joint statement 聯合發表

⊘ **instruction** *n.* [ɪnˋstrʌkʃən] 指示

　同義詞：command, statement, program line

　相關詞：instruction manual 操作指南；instruction execution 指令實施

⊘ **in good order** *ph.* 良好

　同義詞：in the right manner, properly, decently

　相關詞：keep in good order 保持良好

⊘ **in transit** *ph.* 運途中

　同義詞：passing through, during transportation

　相關詞：lost in transit 運途中遺失；damaged in transit 運途中損壞

⊘ **wash away** *ph.* [wɑʃ] 沖走

　同義詞：wash off, remove, take away

　相關詞：wash down 沖洗；washed-out 褪色的

⊘ **overboard** *adv.* [ˋovɚˌbord] （自船上）落水

　相關詞：fell overboard 失足落海；anchor overboard 拋錨入海

⊘ **inclement** *a.* [ɪnˋklɛmənt] 天氣險惡的

　同義詞：rough, stormy, harsh

　相關詞：inclementness，bad weather (n.) 壞天氣

⊘ **insufficient stock** *ph.* 庫存不足

　同義詞：poor stock, short stock, low stock

　相關詞：stock in trade 存貨；stock control 庫存管控

⊘ **production run** *ph.* 投產

　相關詞：pre-production run 試作生產

關鍵句型

I acknowledged the receipt of ...　　確認收到…

例句說明：

· **I hereby acknowledge receipt of** your inquiry of September 9.
特此確認收到貴司九月九日的詢價。

I got a bad/good news with ... to tell.

有件關於…的壞消息/好消息要告知

例句說明：

· The supervisor **got a good news with** the yearly promotion **to tell us**.
主管有件關於年度晉升的好消息要告訴我們。

Owing to …　　由於…

例句說明：

· The fright was cancelled **owing to** torrential rain.
班機因大雨取消了。

英文書信這樣寫

Claim for Shipping Damage with Insurance Company
天然災害索賠（保險公司賠償）

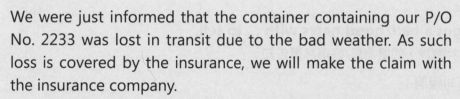

Dear Tony,

We were just informed that the container containing our P/O No. 2233 was lost in transit due to the bad weather. As such loss is covered by the insurance, we will make the claim with the insurance company.

However, as we need the missing lots urgently, it will be highly appreciated if you could arrange immediate production run for us and confirm the earliest delivery date.

Thanks in advance for your prompt attention on this matter.

Sincerely yours,
Tom Smith

－ 中文翻譯 －

湯尼 您好：

我司剛接獲通知，承載我司第2233號訂單的貨櫃因氣象惡劣在運輸途中遺失了。因這項損失屬保險承保的範圍，我們會向保險公司提出索賠。

然而，由於我司急需要此批遺失的貨物，如您能安排立即投產並回覆最快交期，我司將不勝感激。

先感謝您會立即處理此事。

湯姆 史密斯 敬啟

知識補給

　　一般而言，除了不可抗力、貨物本體缺陷及託運人的原因造成的貨物損失外，承運人因自身原因造成的貨物損失均應向貨主負賠償責任。但因運輸慣例、相關的國際公約、海商法均規定了承運人在一定條件下的免責事項，因此，進口商向承運人索賠的範圍大大受限。通常情況下，只有下列原因導致的貨物滅失或損壞，進口商才能向承運人提出索賠要求：

1. 貨物裝卸時發生的損失 (如裝卸不當導致貨物跌落 等)。
2. 積載不當造成的損失 (如輕重貨物不合理堆積 等)
3. 短裝短卸損失 (如承運人的疏失導致裝卸貨物短少 等)。
4. 照料不當造成的損失 (如在運輸途中沒有調節貨艙溫度導致貨物腐爛 等)。
5. 貨物水漬損失 (如貨物遭受海水浸泡而無法使用 等)。但如有投共同海損險則除外。
6. 不合理變更航程造成的損失 (如因變更航程造成船體觸礁、沉沒、互撞等導致貨物損失 等)。
7. 不按規定裝載造成的損失 (如擅自將貨物裝載於甲板上，導致貨物毀損 等)。
8. 其他不能免責的過失導致貨物損失。

　　船公司賠償的事項大約涵蓋下列範圍：

1. **不到貨（non-delivery）**，又稱為 "遺失"，指在船舶正常航行並未遭遇意外事故下，遺失所承載的貨物。
2. **短卸（short landing）**，指在船舶正常航行並未遭遇意外事故下，短卸所承載的貨物。
3. **堆積不當（improper or bad stowage）**，指船艙中堆積不當造成所承載的貨物受損。
4. **處理粗糙（rouge handling）**，指不當裝卸貨物導致所承載的貨物受損。
5. **偷竊（theft and pilferage）**，指貨物在運輸期間遭竊所受的損失。
6. **海水損害（sea water damage）**，指在船舶正常航行並未遭遇意外事故下，所承載的貨物接觸海水所受的損失。

功能瑕疵和數量短出索賠

Claim for function defect and quantity shortage

　　一旦發現功能性產品有功能方面的瑕疵，最快速的解決方式就是尋求製造商的技術人員提供協助，大部分是透過即時書信email或電話和視訊會議獲得解決。對進口商而言，立即在當地解決問題，避免貨物短缺的情況；而對出口商而言，則可避免因品質瑕疵造成的相關費用，例如：不良品退貨運費和換貨之產品成本。

情境說明

Buyer makes claims for quantity shortage with the seller.

買方向賣方提出數量短出索賠。

角色介紹

買方 | Buyer: B, ABC Co., Ltd.

賣方 | Seller: S, Best International Trade Corp.

情境對話

B: Hi, Tony. This is Tom Smith at ABC Co.

B：您好！湯尼，我是ABC 公司的湯姆 史密斯。

S: How are things, Tom?

S：最近可好，湯姆？

B: Just fine. We duly received the shipment against our P/O No. 2255, but found carton No. 2 contains only

B：一切都好。我們剛收到第2255號訂單的貨物，但發現第2號紙箱僅包含10件

10pcs instead of 12pcs as stated in our packing instruction.

S: I have picked up this issue from the survey's report and photos from your QA engineer.

B: As you can tell, the carton stays completed. I'm convinced that it is simply an issue of short shipment.

S: It could be so. The shortage could be caused by unskilled packing by our new staff. I'm truely sorry for the inconvenience caused to you.

B: That is fine, but we must submit our claim for the short shipment.

產品,而不是我們包裝指示要求定的12件。

S: 我已由貴司品保工程師提供的調查報告和照片得知了這個訊息。

B: 您可以看到,紙箱是完整的。我相信這只是單純的短裝問題。

S: 有可能是這樣,可能由於我們的新員工包裝不純熟造成短裝,造成不便我很抱歉。

B: 沒關係,但由於貨物數量短裝,我們必須向你提出索賠。

情境說明

角色介紹

買方 | Buyer: B, ABC Co., Ltd.

賣方 | Seller: S, Best International Trade Corp.

Buyer makes claims for functional defect with the seller.

買方向賣方提出功能瑕疵索賠。

情境對話

B: Hi, Tony. This is Tom Smith at ABC Co. We purchased some new model of valves last month.

B：您好！湯尼，我是 ABC 公司的湯姆 史密斯。上個月我們購買了一些新款閥門。

S: That's right. What do you want to discuss, Tom?

S：沒錯，你想討論什麼呢，湯姆？

B: The product runs into big malfunction problems.

B：這產品有很大的功能障礙問題。

S: Sounds not good. What kind of problems?

S：聽起來不太妙。什麼樣的問題？

B: The valve can't effectively regulate the flow of water, and our engineer can't get the root of the problem.

B：閥門不能有效地調節水流量，而我們的工程師找不出問題的根源。

S: We need you to provide more

S：我們需要您提供更多技術

266

technical support <u>to see if</u> there is any chance to solve this quality problem by ourselves. Otherwise, the relevant expenses and the responsibility <u>should be undertaken by</u> your company.

B: I see. How about having a call to allow our engineer demonstrate how the new valve and accessories to be assembled.

S: Good idea. Just drop me a message whenever you're ready.

訊息援，看看是否能由我們自己解決這個問題。否則，所有費用及責任應由貴司承擔。

B：瞭解。不如開個視訊會議，讓我們的工程師當場示範如何安裝這款新閥門和配件。

S：好主意。只要你準備好了，請馬上與我聯絡。

關鍵字彙

⊘ **survey** *v.* [sə`ve] 觀察；調查測量
同義詞：examine, observe, watch
相關詞：field survey 實地調查

⊘ **QA** *ph.* 品質保證
相關詞：QC, Quality Control 品質控制
解　析：品質保證（Quality Assurance; QA）為確保能滿足品質要求，在品質體系中實施有系統的活動，來證實品質，稱為品質保證。品質保證是以品質控制(Quality Control; QC)為基礎，沒有品質控制，就無法達到品質保證的目的。

⊘ **unskilled** *a.* [ʌn`skɪld] 不熟練的
同義詞：untrained, inexpert, amateur
相關詞：unskilled work 無需技能的工作

⊘ **instead of** *ph.* 寧願

同義詞：in place of, in preference to

相關詞：instead of me 代替我；instead of wasting time 不浪費時間

⊘ **packing instruction** *ph.* 包裝指示

相關詞：packing specification 包裝規格

解　析：包裝指示是指定義產品包裝方式、標準及要求的規範。

⊘ **pick up** *ph.* 獲得

同義詞：gather, obtain, get

相關詞：pick up the tab 替別人付帳；pick up information 獲取資訊

⊘ **regulate** *v.* [`rɛgjəˌlet]　管理、控制、規範

同義詞：adjust, control, manage

相關詞：well-regulated 井然有序的；self-regulated 自動調整的

⊘ **root** *n.* [rut] DJ [ru:t]　根源

同義詞：cause, origin

相關詞：root condition 根本條件，root directory 根目錄

⊘ **demonstrate** *v.* [ˌdɛmənˋstret]　示範，演出

同義詞：exhibition, showing, display

相關詞：demonstration effect 演出效果

⊘ **run into** *ph.* 偶遇，撞到

同義詞：bump into, collide with, come up against

相關詞：run into debt 負債

⊘ **technical support** *ph.* 技術支援

同義詞：tech support, technical help and solutions

相關詞：technical analysis 技術分析；technical superiority 技術優勢

✓ **assemble** *v.* 裝配集合

同義詞：assembly skill, assembly trick

相關詞：assembly fixture 裝配夾具；assembly instruction 裝配指示

關鍵句型

Sb. pick up this issue from ...　由…得知此事

例句說明：

· You can **pick up** some very useful knowledge about trade **from** the senior.

你可從前輩那得到一些真正有用的貿易知識。

As you can tell ...　如你所見…

例句說明：

· **As you can tell**, everything is well done.

如你所見，所有事情都已辦妥了。

to see if ...　看看是否…

例句說明：

· Please check your production schedule **to see if** there's any chance to ship sooner.

請檢視貴司生產排程，看看是否有機會提前出貨。

Sth. should be undertaken by Sb.　應由某人承擔某事

例句說明：

· **This project should be** undertaken **by** our team.

此專案應由我們這組負責。

英文書信這樣寫

Claim for Quantity Shortage 數量短出索賠

Dear Tony,

We received the goods against our P/O No. 2255, but found one carton wasn't full. We think it might have been caused by careless packing.

Please advise if you prefer to make a replacement or refund for the shortage, said 2pcs.

Sincerely yours,
Tom Smith

– 中文翻譯 –

湯尼 你好：

收到貴司所寄送的第2255號訂單的貨物，但發現其中一箱未滿箱。我們認為這是包裝疏失所致。

對於少出的這 2 件，請你補齊，或退款。

湯姆 史密斯 敬啟

知識補給

貨櫃 (Container)的「出口」作業流程：

1. 訂艙：出口商依據合約向船公司或貨物代理辦理訂艙。
2. 簽發裝箱單：確認訂艙後，由船公司簽發裝箱單，發送至貨櫃集散地，安排空櫃和貨運交接。
3. 發送空櫃：整櫃貨所需的空櫃，由船公司送交發貨人，拼櫃貨所需的空櫃通常由貨運站領取。
4. 拼櫃貨裝櫃：貨櫃集散地依據訂艙單核收託運貨物，並簽發貨物收據後，在站內裝櫃。
5. 整櫃貨裝櫃：發貨人收到空櫃後，自行裝櫃並準時送至貨櫃集散地。
6. 貨物交接：站場收據為發貨人發貨和船公司收貨的憑證。
7. 領取提單：發貨人憑站場收據，向船公司領取提單後向銀行結匯。
8. 裝船：貨櫃集散地依據船舶積載計劃，進行裝船發運。

貨櫃（Container）的「進口」作業流程：

1. 貨運單證：憑出口港寄來的有關貨運單證製作。
2. 分發單證：將單證分別送交貨物代理、貨運站和貨櫃集散場。
3. 到貨通知：通知收貨人船舶到港日，準備接貨，並於船舶到港後發出到貨通知。
4. 提單：收貨人依據到貨通知，持正本提單向船公司或貨物代理換取提貨單。
5. 提貨單：船公司或貨物代理核對正本提單無誤後，即簽發提貨單。
6. 提貨：收貨人憑提貨單和進口許可證，至貨櫃集散地辦理領櫃或提貨手續。
7. 整櫃交貨：貨櫃集散地依據提貨單，將貨櫃交由收貨人。
8. 拼櫃交貨：貨運站憑提貨單交貨。

3 包裝不符和裝運延誤索賠
Claim for error packaging and delay shipment

國貿關鍵字 | 貨櫃 |

貨櫃(Container)，是指具有一定強度、剛度和規格，專門在運輸過程中周轉使用的大型裝貨容器。貨櫃上有一組辨識用的11位編號，前四位是字母，後七位是數字，此號碼稱為「櫃號」。

情境說明

Buyer makes claim for error packaging with seller.

買方向賣方提出包裝不符索賠。

角色介紹

買方 | Buyer: B, ABC Co., Ltd.

賣方 | Seller: S, Best International Trade Corp.

情境對話

B: Hello, Tony. This is Tom from ABC Co.

B：你好，湯尼，我是ABC有限公司的湯姆。

S: Hi, Tom. I'm just going to call you about your P/O No. 9900.

S：您好！湯姆，我正要打給你討論您的第9900號訂單。

B: That's exact why I'm calling for. The

B：這正是我打給您的原因。

parts we received are packed in cardboard carton directly without wrapping cotton paper. That's different from our instruction.

我們收到的產品直接裝在硬紙箱內，沒有使用棉紙包裝，這與我們的指示不同。

S: The error might be caused by the oversight of Packing Department. We'll make quality investigation to identify the corrective action plan.

S：這可能是包裝部疏忽所造成的錯誤，我們會進行品質調查，以找出改善行動方案。

B: Due to such error, repackaging must be conducted before delivering to our customers.

B：由於此包裝錯誤，出貨給客戶前須再重新包裝。

S: I'm terribly sorry for any inconvenience caused by the error packaging.

S：很抱歉因的包裝造成您的不便。

B: We have to lodge a claim against you for the error packing, even though we are unwilling to do so.

B：雖然不願意這樣做，但我們仍然要向貴司提出包裝錯誤的賠償要求。

273

情境說明

Buyer makes claim for delayed shipment with seller.

買方向賣方提出裝運延誤索賠。

情境對話

B: Hi, Tony. This is Tom Smith calling from ABC Co.

S: How are things, Tom?

B: Not bad. With regret that we have to lodge a claim against you for the late delivery of our P/O No. 3366.

S: We had notified you about the postponement and thought you could accept the rescheduled shipment.

B: That's true. However, as the lots failed our incoming inspection, we spent three days implementing 100% inspection to sort out the faulty parts.

B：您好！湯尼，我是ABC公司的湯姆 史密斯。

S：近來可好，湯姆？

B：還可以，但很遺憾我們不得不針對貴司延遲交貨我司第3366號訂單的交貨期提出索賠。

S：我們已通知貴司關於訂單延遲，以為貴司能接受重新安排裝運。

B：沒錯。但這批貨未通過我們的進貨檢驗，所以我們花了三天時間來執行完整檢驗，以找出故障品。

274

S: <u>Please</u> pardon <u>us for</u> the late shipment and unexpected quality defect.

S：請原諒我們延遲裝運及非預期的品質瑕疵問題。

B: Owing to the additional inspection time, we were unable to fulfill customers' orders. <u>We have no alternative but</u> to press a claim with you for compensation.

B：有鑑於額外的檢驗時間使得我們無法即時履行客戶訂單。我們別無選擇，只能向貴司提出索賠。

關鍵字彙

⊘ **wrap** *v.* [ræp] 包，裹
同義詞：bag, package, cover
相關詞：wrap up 打包好；wrapped up in 被包裹於

⊘ **identify** *v.* [aɪˋdɛntəˌfaɪ] 確認；鑑定
同義詞：recognize, evaluate, key out
相關詞：identify oneself 自稱；identify oneself with 參與

⊘ **conduct** *v.* [kənˋdʌkt] 引導，帶領
同義詞：direct, guide, lead
相關詞：conduct oneself 表現沉著；conduct of trial 進行試驗

⊘ **corrective** *a.* [kəˋrɛktɪv] 改正的
同義詞：remedial, improving, rectifying
相關詞：corrective control 校正控制；corrective element 校正元素

⊘ **contrary to** *ph.* 與之相反
同義詞：as opposite to, counter to

相關詞：contrary to expectation 與預期相反；contrary to company philosophy 與公司理念相左

⊘ **cotton paper** *ph.* 棉紙

相關詞：carbon paper 複寫紙

⊘ **reschedule** *v.* [ri`skɛdʒʊl] 重新安排時間

同義詞：make a new timetable, set a new time and date

相關詞：reschedule the shipment 重新安排出貨；

　　　reschedule the meeting 重新安排會議

⊘ **faulty** *a.* [`fɔltɪ] 有缺點的，不完美的

同義詞：defective, imperfect

相關詞：faulty packing of cargo 貨物包裝不良

⊘ **incoming inspection** *ph.* 進料檢驗

同義詞：receiving inspection

相關詞：outgoing inspection 出貨檢驗

⊘ **100% inspection** *ph.* 全檢，百百檢

相關詞：sampling, random check 抽檢；AQL (Acceptable Quality Levels) 合格品質水準

解　析：AQL為驗貨時的依據，為國際標準，定義批量範圍、抽樣數量及相對應的合格與不合格產品的數量。

關鍵句型

The error might be caused by ...　此錯誤可能導因於

例句說明：

· **The error might be caused by** failure in cross-departmental communication.
　此錯誤可能導因於跨部門溝通失效。

Sb. have to …, even though Sb. be unwilling to do so.
雖然不願，但某人仍必須…

例句說明：

· The manager **has to** accept his resignation, **even though she is unwilling to do so**.
　雖然不願，但經理得同意他的辭呈。

Please pardon Sb. for ...　請原諒某人…

例句說明：

· **Please pardon me for** the late reply.
　請原諒我延遲回覆。

Sb. have no alternative but to ...　某人別無選擇只能…

例句說明：

· The manager **has no alternative but to** accept her resignation.
　經理別無選擇只能接受她的辭呈。

英文書信這樣寫

Claim for Delay Shipment 裝運延誤索賠

Dear Tony,

This is to notify you that the delay of our P/O No. 3366 has disappointed us, especially the fact that we have not been given any explanation for the delay.

In accordance with our contract, the lots should have arrived at our port before July 7; however, we haven't received them yet.

Due to the delay, we weren't able to meet the commitment to our customers. We shall ask you being responsible for our losses caused by the delay.

Please arrange the delivery as soon as possible, as we won't accept the delay any more.

Sincerely yours,
Tom Smith

－ 中文翻譯 －

湯尼 您好：

在此通知貴司，我司第3366號訂單的延遲情形讓我們備感失望，尤其是貴司尚未提供任何合理的解釋。

依據合約，此批貨應在七月七日前運抵我方港口，但截至目前，我司仍未收到貨物。因您的延遲交貨，使我失違背對客戶的承諾。此延誤所致的一切損失都將歸究於貴司。

請貴司儘速交貨，我司將無法再接受有任何的延遲。

湯姆 史密斯 敬啟

知識補給

貨櫃主要分類：

1. 依裝載貨物別: 雜貨櫃、散貨櫃、液體貨櫃、冷藏貨櫃等。
2. 依貨櫃材質別: 合金貨櫃，鋼板貨櫃，纖維板貨櫃，玻璃鋼貨櫃等。
3. 依貨櫃結構別: 摺疊式貨櫃、固定式貨櫃（包括密閉貨櫃、開頂貨櫃、板架貨櫃等）等。
4. 依貨櫃重量別: 30噸貨櫃、20噸貨櫃、10噸貨櫃、5噸貨櫃、2.5噸貨櫃等。
5. 依貨櫃規格別: 國際上一般使用的貨櫃規格有20呎櫃、40呎櫃、40呎高櫃、45呎高櫃、20呎開頂櫃、40呎開頂櫃、20呎平底貨櫃、40呎平底貨櫃等。
6. 依貨櫃用途別: 乾貨櫃（Dry Container）、冷凍貨櫃（Reefer Container）、掛衣貨櫃（Dress Hanger Container）、開頂貨櫃（Open Top Container）、框架貨櫃（Flat Rack Container）、罐式貨櫃（Tank Container）等。

職場經驗談

　　安排出貨人員需事先計算貨物的材積，尤其是出整櫃貨時，決定所需要貨櫃規格，避免貨櫃無法一次性承載所有貨物，或裝載後未滿櫃的情形發生。因此，貨櫃規格及其尺寸即為重要的參考依據，以最常見的20英呎貨櫃為例，其尺寸為20英呎長 x 8英尺寬 x 8.5英呎高，體積相當於1360立方英呎（39 m³）。

材積計算說明：

　　一材＝1 Cuft （1 Cubic Feet 立方呎）＝長×寬× 高（公分）×0.0000353, 1 立方米 (Cubic Meter, CBM) / 35.315 Cuft（立方呎）

　　一般來說，一個20呎貨櫃約可裝26~28個CBM，而40呎貨櫃約可裝56～58個CBM。

關證延誤和付款延遲索賠

Claim for Suspended Import Documents with Seller and Delayed Payment with Buyer

國貿關鍵字 │ 延遲付款 │

一般來說，買賣雙方在交易之初會在合約中定義付款期限，如買方因故無法在期限內履行支付款項的承諾，則賣方會追討未收的應收帳款，這個行為即為「逾期應收帳款管理」。為了避免面臨帳款無法追收的風險，而成為呆帳，因此買賣雙方開始交易前，進行的信用調查就是相當重要的一環。

情境說明

Seller makes a claim for suspended import documents with buyer.

賣方公司向買方公司提出進口文件延誤索賠。

角色介紹

買方 │ Buyer: B, ABC Co., Ltd.

賣方 │ Seller: S, Best International Trade Corp.

情境對話

B: Hi, Tony. This is Tom Smith calling from ABC Co.

B：您好，湯尼，我是ABC公司的湯姆 史密斯。

S: Hello, Tom. What's up?

S：您好，湯姆，你好嗎？

B: Not bad. I'm calling to express I am deeply sorry that we still haven't been able to open the L/C and pick

B：我打來是要對我司到目前仍無法開出信用狀及提貨，向您表達深摯的歉

up the cargo so far.

意。

S: What happened? I thought you said everything was going well.

S：發生什麼事了嗎？我以為您說過一切進展順利。

B: I did. Everything was done but the import license. We still haven't obtain it.

B：我是說過。一切都完成了，除了進口許可證還沒拿到。

S: That's extremely terrible. <u>How are you going to</u> solve the problem?

S：這真是太糟了！你打算如何解決這問題？

B: It seems that the condition hasn't taken a favorable turn. We have no choice but to terminate the contract.

B：看來情況似乎尚未出現轉機，我們別無選擇，只能中止合約。

S: In this case, we will make the claim with you based on the clauses on termination or cancellation of contract.

S：在此情形下，我司將根據契約終止或解除的規定，向貴司提出索賠。

Seller makes a claim for delayed payment with seller.

賣方向買方提出付款延遲索賠。

角色介紹

買方｜Buyer: B, ABC Co., Ltd.

賣方｜Seller: S, Best International Trade Corp.

情境對話

S: Hello, Tom. This is Tony Yang at Best Co.

S：你好，湯姆，我是倍斯特公司的湯尼 楊。

B: Hi, Tony. What can I do for you?

B：您好！湯尼，有什麼能為您效勞的地方？

S: I'm calling to remind you that we still haven't received the payment against your P/O No. 9900 after repeated reminders.

S：我打來提醒您，我們一再提醒，但仍未收到貴司第9900號訂單的付款。

B: I'm very sorry for the late remittance.

B：非常抱歉延遲匯款。

S: Could you let me know what the problem is?

S：能讓我知道是什麼問題嗎？

B: Shortage of money was a large part of the problem. Please grant us one more week to transfer the money to

B：資金不足是主要問題，請寬限我們一個星期，在下週末之前會轉帳給您。

you by next weekend.

S: If this is the case, we cannot but claim on you for the recovery of our loss by deducting half of your commission.

S：如果是這樣，我們不得不以扣掉一半佣金的方式向貴司索賠，以賠償我們的損失。

B: Is there any compromise?

B：有任何轉圜餘地嗎？

S: That is probably the only way we can accept.

S：那大概是我們可以接受的唯一途徑。

關鍵字彙

⊘ **terminate** *v.* [ˋtɝmə͵net] 使停止，使結束

同義詞：end, conclude, discontinue

相關詞：to terminate Sb. 解雇某人，terminate the visit 結束拜訪

⊘ **termination** *n.* [͵tɝməˋneʃən] 停止，結束

同義詞：end, conclusion, completion

相關詞：termination of employment 終止雇用，termination of insurance 保險終止

⊘ **clause** *n.* [klɔz] 條款

同義詞：article, item, paragraph

同義詞：clause rider 附加條款，clause of no effect 無效條款

⊘ **go well** *ph.* 進展順利

同義詞：succeed, pass over nicely, go on smoothly

相關詞：go badly, work out badly, to be unsuccessful 進展不順

⊘ **import license** *ph.* 進口許可證

相關詞：import duty 進口稅，import-export trade 進出口貿易

解　析：進口許可證是指進口國家規定進口某些商品必須事先取得許可證。

⊘ **favorable turn** *ph.* 轉機

同義詞：promising change, advantageous development

相關詞：favorable case 有利情形，favorable condition 優惠條件

⊘ **remittance** *n.* [rɪ`mɪtns] 匯款

同義詞：sending of a payment, remitting money

相關詞：foreign remittance, overseas remittance 海外匯款

⊘ **recovery** *n.* [rɪ`kʌvərɪ] 重獲，復原

同義詞：recuperation, getting well, return

相關詞：recovery factor 回收率，recovery procedure 恢復過程

⊘ **deduct** *v.* [kouchu] 扣除

同義詞：subtract, tale off

相關詞：deductible franchise 可扣除的免賠額

⊘ **repeating reminder** *ph.* 重複提醒

同義詞：continual reminding message

相關詞：reminder of the bill 催繳單

⊘ **shortage of money** *ph.* 資金短缺

同義詞：lack of money, shortage of finances

相關詞：turnover of capital 資金周轉，debt crisis 債務危機

⊘ **transfer the money** *ph.* 轉帳

同義詞：transfer the amount

相關詞：bank transfer 銀行轉帳

關鍵句型

Sb. still haven't been able to ...　某人仍無法…

例句說明：

- **We still haven't been able to** get used to the new operating system.
  我們仍然無法習慣新作業系統。

How are you going to ...　你將如何…

例句說明：

- **How are you going to** fix the situation of tight production capacity?
  你將如何解決產能吃緊的情形？

Sth. be a large part of the problem ...　某物為造成…的主要問題

例句說明：

- Inexperience **is a large part of the problem** making him inefficient.
  經驗不足是造成他工作效率低的主要問題。

Please grant Sb. ... for　請寬限/容許某人…

例句說明：

- **Please grant me** five minutes **for** taking a break.
  請容許我休息五分鐘。

英文書信這樣寫

Claim for Delayed Payment
付款延遲索賠

Dear Tony,

We are very sorry for the late remittance of our payment. I'm writing to express our deep regret.

The main reason for bringing about this situation was that the sales was lower than expected. We will transfer the amount to you by this weekend, and you can be sure that such a delay won't happen again.

Appreciate your understanding.

Sincerely yours,
Tom Smith

– 中文翻譯 –

湯尼 您好：
非常抱歉我司的匯款延遲了。在此向您表達我司的歉意。
主要是因市場銷售不如預期所造成。我們會在本週末前匯款給您，並保證匯款延遲將不再發生。
還請您諒解。
湯姆 史密斯 敬啟

知識補給

　　資金短缺（**shortage of finances**）是指企業所擁有的資金量少於維持企業正常營運所需要的資金量。資金為企業持續經營的必要條件，若資金短缺，又不能及時籌措，輕者將致使企業無法繼續商業活動，如採購生產原料，生產停擺、停工等，重者將使企業償債能力下降，造成債務危機，進而影響企業信譽。

　　償債能力（**debt-paying ability**）是指企業償還到期債務的承受能力或保證程度，包括償還短期債務和長期債務的能力，為企業能否持續生存和發展的關鍵。因此，企業償債能力是評估企業財務狀況和經營能力的重要指標。

Notes 筆記欄

要求補貨和換貨
Request of Replenishment and Replacement

國貿關鍵字 | 補貨和換貨 |

　　出錯貨的狀況是難免的，但因賣方無法確定客人何時會回報出錯貨物的狀況，這時需要特別注意是否會產生延遲交貨違約的問題，有些客戶會以收到正確零件的日期算起。處理退換貨的重點是須注意延誤交期的罰金和多次往返的寄送費用可能會導致利潤的折損。

情境說明

Buyer requests seller to replenish the shortage of consignment.

買方公司要求賣方對短缺的貨進行補貨。

角色介紹

買方 | Buyer: B, ABC Co., Ltd.

賣方 | Seller: S, Best International Trade Corp.

情境對話

B: Hi, Tony. This is Tom Smith at ABC Co.

B：您好！湯尼，我是ABC公司的湯姆 史密斯。

S: How may I help you, Tom?

S：需要什麼協助嗎，湯姆？

B: The shipment of our P/O No. 5678 arrived yesterday, but our inspector found pallet No. 2 contains only 30

B：我司第5678號訂單的這批貨已於昨天運抵，但我們檢查員發現2號棧板僅包含

cartons instead of 31.

30 箱貨而不是 31箱。

S: I have been advised of this matter through the Certificate of Inspection.

S：我已從檢驗證書中發現這件事。

B: As you can tell, the PE films covering around the pallet stays completed. I'm convinced that it is simply an issue of short shipment.

B：您可看到的，覆蓋在棧板周圍的PE膜是完整。我想這只是一個單純的短裝問題。

S: It could be so. The shortage could be caused by our unskilled new staff. Really sorry for the inconvenience caused to you, Tom.

S：有可能是這樣，可能是由於我們的新員工包裝不純熟造成短缺。造成您的不便，我很抱歉，湯姆。

B: That is fine, but we must submit our claim for the shortage of goods.

B：沒關係，但我們必須對貨物的短缺索賠。

S: Please advise if you prefer to make up the difference or refund.

S：請問貴司傾向補足差異數量或退款。

B: Please make the replenishment for the shortage.

B：請補足不足數量。

情境說明

Buyer requests seller to replace the faulty consignment.

買方要求賣方換掉異常的貨物。

角色介紹

買方 | Buyer: B, ABC Co., Ltd.

賣方 | Seller: S, Best International Trade Corp.

情境對話

B: Hi, Tony. This is Tom Smith at ABC Co. Did you try to reach me earlier?

B：您好！湯尼，我是 ABC 公司的湯姆 史密斯。你稍早找我嗎？

S: That's right. With reference to our video conference call this Monday, have you reassembled the new valve as demonstrated by our engineer?

S：沒錯。關於星期一我們在視訊會議中所討論的事，您是否已經依我司工程師展示的操作方法重新組裝新款閥門呢？

B: We just finished 100% sorting and functionality testing and found 52pcs out of 2,000pcs still can't function.

B：我們剛完成了100%分類和功能測試，並從2000件中發現52件仍無法運作。

S: Sounds bad. Sincerely sorry for our careless examination on the parts.

S：聽起來真糟。很抱歉我們在檢驗上有疏忽。

B: You're asked to exchange the faulty parts at once by express at your cost.

B：我們要求由您付費安排快遞，立即對所有故障的產品進行換貨。

S: No problem. I'll arrange the delivery as quick as possible. In the meanwhile, please return the non-conforming parts for rework.

S：沒問題。我會盡快安排出貨。在此同時，請退回不合格產品讓我們維修。

B: Besides, <u>as the responsibility rests with your firm, the additional sorting fee and testing fee should be undertaken by you as well.</u>

B：此外，因這次品質問題的責任在貴公司，額外的全檢費用和測試費用亦應由貴司支付。

S: Naturally. Please send us the debit note for the relevant expenses caused.

S：當然。再請將所有相關費用的欠款單寄給我們。

關鍵字彙

⊘ **inspector** *n.* [ɪn`spɛktɚ] 檢查員

同義詞：censor, examiner

相關詞：inspector of taxes 稅務員；inspector general 檢察長

⊘ **refund** *n.* [rɪ`fʌnd] 退還，退款

同義詞：repayment, return of money, reimbursement

相關詞：refundment 退還；退款的行為

⊘ **replenishment** *n.* [rɪ`plɛnɪʃmənt] 再裝滿；補充；充滿

同義詞：resupplying, refilling, renewal

相關詞：stock replenishment，inventory replenishment 補充庫存

⊘ **pallet** *n.* [`pælɪt] 棧板

相關詞：pallet conveyor 棧板輸送帶

解　析：棧板為用於集裝、堆放、搬運和運輸貨物的水平平臺裝置，棧板為物流運作過程中重要的裝卸、儲存和運輸設備，現今已廣泛應用於生產、運輸、倉儲和流通等領域。

⊘ **short-shipped** *ph.* 短裝

同義詞：short shipment

相關詞：overloaded 溢裝

⊘ **make up** *ph.* 補足

同義詞：supplement, replenish

相關詞：make up for 補償；make up the sum 補足總數

⊘ **reassemble** *v.* [riə`sɛmb!] 重組

同義詞：gather again, put together again, reconvene

相關詞：reassemble remaining spare parts 重組剩餘的備用零件

⊘ **function** *v. n.* [`fʌŋkʃən] 作用，運作

同義詞：work, operate, perform

相關詞：multi-function 多功能的；quality management function 品質管理職能

⊘ **examination** *n.* [ɪɡ͵zæmə`neʃən] 檢查

同義詞：inspection, test, experiment

相關詞：examination of product 產品檢驗；examination work 檢驗工作

⊘ **non-conforming** *a.* 不合格的

同義詞：unqualified, off-grade

相關詞：non-conforming materials 不合格的物料；non-conforming process 不合格的流程

⊘ **debit note** *ph.* 欠款單，借項通知單

同義詞：debit memo

相關詞：debit balance 借方餘額；debit interest 欠息

關鍵句型

Sb. have been advised of ... 某人已被通知

例句說明：

- **The buyer has been advised of** the shipment delay.
  買家已獲知出貨延遲的消息。
- **She has been advised of** her promotion.
  獲得晉升一事，她已接到通知了。

Sb. be convinced that ... 某人相信

例句說明：

- **I am convinced that** the customer will accept this new style.
  我相信客戶會接受這個新款式。
- **She is convinced that** her performance is better than others.
  她相信自己表現優於其它人。

Sb. be asked to ... 要求某人

例句說明：

- The manufacturer **is asked to do** out-going inspection.
  製造商須做出貨檢驗。

As the responsibility rests with Sb., …should be undertaken by Sb. as well. 責任歸屬在於某人，亦應由某人承擔…

例句說明：

- **As the responsibility** of cargo lost **rests with** the shipping company, the loss **should be undertaken by** them company as well.
  貨物遺失的責任屬於船公司，損失亦應由其承擔。

Request of Replacement 要求換貨

Dear Tony,

The shipment of our P/O No. 5678 arrived this morning. All the parts seem to be in good condition; however, there's a problem in assembling some of the parts with the connectors.

After conducting 100% assembly test, 52pcs out of 2,000pcs failed. Please arrange the replacement for the said quantities at once.

Your early reply would be appreciated.

Sincerely yours,
Tom Smith

– 中文翻譯 –

湯尼 您好：

我司訂購的第5678號訂單貨物已於今早抵達，所有貨物看來都良好，但是有些與連接管裝配時出現問題。

在進行100%組裝測試後，發現這2,000件產品中有52件不合格，請立即安排補出這些數量更換產品。

若您能早日回覆，我司將不勝感激。

湯姆 史密斯 敬啟

知識補給

商品檢驗證書（**Commodity Inspection Certificate**）：

進出口商品經過商檢機構檢驗後，由該檢驗機構所出具的書面檢驗證明稱為「商品檢驗證書」。也可由生產單位，即製造商自行檢驗後出具檢驗報告，此類報告也可視為檢驗證書的一種。商品檢驗證書的作用主要有：

1. 為賣方所交付貨物的品質、重量、數量、包裝等是否符合合約規定的依據。
2. 當貨物存在爭議時，為買方對品質、數量、重量、包裝等提出拒收，並要求賠償的憑證。
3. 為記載貨物在裝卸時及運輸中的實際狀況，當貨物存在爭議時，為釐清責任歸屬的依據。
4. 為買賣雙方交接貨物、結算貨款和處理索賠的主要憑證。
5. 為繳付關稅、結算運費的憑證。
3. 為賣方向銀行議付貨款的單據。

職場經驗談

在國際貿易中，檢驗機構可為國家設置的檢驗單位，或經由政府註冊的獨立檢驗公司，兩者的作用都是在對進出口的商品的裝運、質量、規格、包裝、數量、重量、衛生、安全、檢疫、殘損等進行檢驗和監督管理。進出口商品檢驗是貨物移轉過程中不可或缺的一個步驟。檢驗合格者，發給檢驗證書，出口商即可依此進行報關；檢驗不合格者，可申請複驗，複驗仍不合格者，則不得出口。

4
買賣、運輸、保險賠償

295

要求退貨和要求退款
Request of Return and Refund

國貿關鍵字 | 退貨 |

　　商品的品質不佳、送錯貨物或規格有問題都是主要造成退貨的原因。因為貨物的退貨會牽涉到協商賠償的問題，較容易產生爭議，如果是商品品質問題，基本上會請買方提供照片和相關數據文件支持出口商的講法。如預算許可，也有公司會聘僱檢測人員到當地驗貨。

情境說明

Buyer requests to return the consignment with error packaging to seller.

買方公司要求將包裝錯誤的貨物退回給賣方公司。

角色介紹

買方 | Buyer: B, ABC Co., Ltd.

賣方 | Seller: S, Best International Trade Corp.

情境對話

B: Hello, Tony. This is Tom from ABC Co.

B：你好，湯尼，我是ABC 公司的湯姆。

S: Hi, Tom. What can I do for you today?

S：您好！湯姆，有什麼能為您效勞的地方？

B: What I'd like to bring up is the packaging of our P/O No. 9900.

B：我想討論的是關於我司第9900號訂單的包裝。

S: Anything wrong?

B: The lots we received were found mislabeled outside the inner box.

S: I'm very sorry for the packaging error. The error might result from the deferred input and maintenance of up-to-date computerized records.

B: Due to such an error, we must return whole batch to your London branch for repackaging. Delivery costs will have to be borne by your side.

S: I see.

B: Besides, we'll have to request a US$500 compensation because your unavailable supply in time.

S：有什麼問題嗎？

B：我們收到的這批貨內盒標籤錯誤。

S：對錯誤包裝我很抱歉。該錯誤可能因為未即時輸入最新的電腦記錄。

B：由於此錯誤，我們必須將整批貨退回貴司的倫敦分部重新包裝，其運費得由你們來負擔。

S：瞭解。

B：此外，因無法即時供應我們需求，我們得向您請求賠償500美元的損失。

情境說明

角色介紹
買方｜Buyer: B, ABC Co., Ltd.
賣方｜Seller: S, Best International Trade Corp.

Buyer requests seller to refund an incorrect shipment.

因為賣方送錯貨，買方要求退款。

情境對話

B: Hi, Tony. This is Tom Smith calling from ABC Co.

B：您好！湯尼，我是ABC 公司的湯姆 史密斯。

S: How are things, Tom?

S：近來可好，湯姆？

B: So so. With regret that we have to lodge a claim against you for the shipment of our P/O No. 3366 we just received.

B：馬馬虎虎。很遺憾我們對剛收到的第3366號訂單，要向您提出索賠。

S: We had notified you about the postponement and thought you could accept the rescheduled shipment.

S：我們已經通知您此批出貨會延遲，以為您能接受重新安排的交期。

B: That's true. However, upon unpacking all of the cartons, we found they didn't contain the goods we ordered.

B：沒錯。然而打開所有的紙箱後，我們發現箱內所裝的貨並非我們訂購的產品。

S: That's too terrible. It's probably that the goods were shipped mistakenly as the result of inadequately training of new staff. Sincerely sorry for our negligence.

B: We will return the goods to you and demand a refund.

S：那真是太糟糕了！送錯貨可能是新進人員缺乏訓練。很抱歉有這樣的疏失。

B：我們將退回貨品，並要求退款。

關鍵字彙

⊘ **maintenance** *n.* [`mentənəns] 維持，保持
同義詞：preservation, upkeep, servicing
相關詞：maintenance cost 保養費；maintenance man 維修員

⊘ **computerize** *v.* [kəm`pjutəˌraɪz] 使電腦化
同義詞：computerise
相關詞：computerised system 電腦化系統

⊘ **borne** *pp.* [born] 承擔（bear的過去分詞）
同義詞：hold, withstand, endure
相關詞：bear up 支持；bear with 忍受

⊘ **bring up** *ph.* 提出討論
同義詞：raise up, discuss
相關詞：bring off 經營成功；bring on 引起

⊘ **mislabel** *v.* 貼錯標籤
同義詞：label incorrectly
相關詞：mislabeled, misbranded 貼錯標的

299

⊘ **up-to-date** *a.* [`ʌptə`det] 最新的

同義詞：recent, latest

相關詞：up-to-date information 最新訊息；keep me up-to-date 告知我最新進展

⊘ **unpack** *v.* [ʌn`pæk] 打開（包裹等）取出東西

同義詞：unload, take out, bring out

相關詞：unpacking the clothes 打開行李取出衣服，packing and unpacking process 裝拆箱流程

⊘ **mistakenly** *adv.* [mɪ`stekənlɪ] 錯誤地；被誤解地

同義詞：accidentally, unintentionally

相關詞：to believe mistakenly 誤信，to think mistakenly 誤以為

⊘ **inadequate** *adj.* [ɪn`ædəkwɪtlɪ] 不適當地

同義詞：unsatisfactorily, insufficiently improper

相關詞：be inadequately prepared 準備不全

⊘ **train** *v.* [tren] 訓練

同義詞：instruct, coach

相關詞：nature and train 教養，trainee 受訓學員

⊘ **return** *v.* [rɪ`tɝn] 返回，退還

同義詞：send back, give back

相關詞：return visit 回訪；a return journey 來回行程

⊘ **new staff** *ph.* 新進員工

同義詞：newcomer, freshman, entrant

相關詞：a newcomer to the neighborhood 新來的鄰居

關鍵句型

What I'd like to bring up is ...　我想要提出討論的是…

例句說明：

· **What I'd like to bring up is** the preventive action for recurrence of quality issue.

我想要討論的是如何避免再有品質問題發生的措施。

Sb. will have to ...　某人將必須…

例句說明：

· **Supervisors will have to** attend the interdepartmental meeting tomorrow morning.

主管將須參加明天早上的跨部門會議。

have notified Sb. about ...　通知某人有關於

例句說明：

· The factory **has notified** customers **about** the holiday calendar of next year.

製造商已通知客戶明年的休假日程表。

as the result of　某事由於

例句說明：

· He failed **as the result of** serious miscalculation.

他因為嚴重的計算錯誤而失敗了。

Request of Return and Refund 要求退貨及退款

Dear Tony,

Please be informed that the goods we received against our P/O No. 3366 is not the type we ordered. I am afraid that you shipped the wrong goods.

I'll return the goods to you and ask for a refund.

Sincerely yours,
Tom Smith

─ 中文翻譯 ─

湯尼 您好:

在此通知貴司,已收到的第3366號訂單的貨物並非我司所訂購的型號。恐怕貴司把貨物寄錯了。

我司將安排退貨並要求退款。

湯姆 史密斯 敬啟

知識補給

　　包裝(**Package**),是指在運輸過程中用以保護產品、方便儲存,利於裝載、促進產品銷售,所使用的容器、材料及物品等。依其功能別,包裝大致可分為商業包裝及工作包裝兩大類:

1. 商業包裝: 是以促進產品銷售為目的的包裝,因此這種包裝著重於外形美觀,目的在於適合商店陳列及能吸引顧客購買等。

2. 工業包裝: 又稱為 "運輸包裝"，是產品在運輸及物流過程中所需的必要包裝，目的在於保護商品、便於儲存及裝載等。在堅固包裝能保護產品的前提下，工業包裝的費用越低則越能達到最佳的成本效益。

　　紙箱（**Carton**），是使用最廣泛的包裝方式，其最常被使用的又屬瓦楞紙箱。瓦楞紙板是由面紙、裡紙、芯紙和加工成波形瓦楞的瓦楞紙粘合而成，加工後可分為單面瓦楞紙板、三層瓦楞紙板、五層、七層、十一層等。

　　不同波紋形狀的瓦楞紙板，其功能也有所不同。目前國際上通用的瓦楞楞形分

職場經驗談

　　包裝的目的之一在於保護產品於運送及流通過程中不致毀損，因此常會在包裝外箱上備註警告標語。

實務上常用的英文警告標語如下：

Keep dry 保持乾燥	Fragile 易碎品
Keep cool 保持低溫	Perishable 易壞品
Keep away from fire 遠離火源	Glass with care 小心玻璃
Heave here 此處舉起	Poison 小心中毒
Open here 此處開啟	Do not drop 小心掉落
Sling here 此處懸索	Guard against wet 勿使受潮
This side up 此面朝上	No smoking 嚴禁煙火
Handle with care 小心搬運	Keep flat 注意平放
Inflammable 易燃物	Keep upright 注意豎放

取消訂單
Request of Order Cancellation

國貿關鍵字 │ 生產能力 │

　　生產能力(Production Capacity)，簡稱產能，是指在一定生產計劃期間，製造者，製造者所能投入生產的相關軟硬體設備、固定資產，及技術能力等條件下，所能產出的產品數量。因此產能即代表製造者的生產規模，當需求大時，需評估增加產能的必要性，避免產能吃緊；反之，當需求小時，則需要考慮縮小規模，以避免產能過剩和降低損失。

情境說明

The buyer requests to cancel the order placed to the seller due to the postponed shipment.

因賣方公司出貨延遲，買方要求取消訂單。

角色介紹

買方│Buyer: B, ABC Co., Ltd.

賣方│Seller: S, Best International Trade Corp.

情境對話

S: Hello, Tom. I'm returning your call.

B: Hello, Tony, In regard to the delayed shipment of our P/O No. 7788, several emails were sent to you to follow up the status, but you deferred the response.

S：你好，湯姆。我打來是要回電給您。

B：你好，湯尼。關於我司第7788號訂單延遲裝運事宜，發了多封 email 給您跟蹤進度，但遲遲未收到您的回覆。

S: I am deeply sorry for not replying you in time. We're trying to coordinate with customers to resolve capacity conflict issue.

S：很抱歉沒能即時回覆您。我們正試著與客戶協調，解決產能衝突問題。

B: Are you making any progress?

B：有任何進展嗎？

S: Not just yet.

S：還沒有

B: As your shipment delay will make us passing up the upcoming sales season, we have no choice but to cancel the order.

B：因為您出貨延遲將使我們錯過即將來的銷售旺季。我們將被迫要取消訂單。

S: Sorry that we can't agree the order cancellation, as most of these customized items were finished and the remaining are in WIP.

S：很抱歉，我們不能取消訂單，因為此批客製化產品大多數都已完成，剩餘的也在生產中。

B: If this is the case, we can only take the finished parts, and absorb the scrap of WIP.

B：如果是這樣，我們只能接受成品，並吸收在製品報廢。

情境說明

The buyer requests to cancel the order placed to the seller due to the production postponement.

因賣方公司生產延遲，買方要求取消訂單。

角色介紹

買方 | Buyer: B, ABC Co., Ltd.

賣方 | Seller: S, Best International Trade Corp.

情境對話

S: Hello, Tom. I'm returning your call.

S：你好，湯姆，我打來是要回電給您。

B: Hello, Tony. I've tried to phone you several times to follow up the production status of our P/O No. 9090. Did your secretary leave a message for you, didn't she?

B：你好，湯尼，我試著打了幾次電話給您，要追縱我司第9090號訂單的生產狀態。您的秘書沒留言給您嗎？

S: My apologies for not replying you in time. I were occupied with internal production meeting.

S：抱歉未即時回覆您。我剛剛在會議中。

B: Any updates can be shared with me?

B：有任何更新進度嗎？

S: Our production came to a standstill due to the worse shortage of raw materials. What is worse; the supplier

S：由於缺少原料，我們的生產也停頓了。更糟的是，供應商也不能確定實際交貨日。

can't be certain of the delivery date.

B: That's too terrible. Your production situation might cause us failing to fulfill customers' demand. If so, we are obliged to cancel the order.

B：這太糟糕了。貴司的生產情況可能會導致我們無法滿足客戶的需求。如果是這樣，我們必須取消訂單。

S: Sorry to bear that We can not but respect your decision regretfully.

S：很遺憾聽到貴司的決定是如此，但我們只能給予尊重了。

關鍵字彙

◎ **defer** *v.* [dɪˋfɝ] 推遲，使展期
同義詞：delay, postpone, put off
相關詞：deferred payment 延期付款；deferred tax 遞延稅項

◎ **resolve** *v.* [rɪˋzɑlv] 解決，解答
同義詞：settle, solve, find a solution
相關詞：resolve the crisis 解決危機；resolve problem 解決問題

◎ **return Sb.'s call** *ph.* 回電
同義詞：ring Sb.'s bank, phone Sb.'s back
相關詞：write back 回信

◎ **coordinate** *v.* [koˋɔrdnɪt] 協調
同義詞：arrange, organize, set up
相關詞：coordinate the work of the department 協調部門工作

⊘ **pass up** *ph.* 拒絕，放棄

同義詞：miss, give up on, forego

相關詞：pass up the chance 錯過機會；never pass up 決不放棄

⊘ **customized item** *ph.* 客製化產品

同義詞：personalized goods, custom-built product

相關詞：customized service 客製化服務；customized propose 客製化方案

⊘ **standstill** *n.* [`stænd͵stɪl] 停滯不前

同義詞：stop, halt, pause,

相關詞：standstill on the expressway 高速公路陷於癱瘓

⊘ **certain** *v. adj.* [`sɝtən] 確定

同義詞：definite, determined, fixed

相關詞：a certain person 某人；be certain about 肯定, 確定

⊘ **situation** *n.* [͵sɪtʃʊ`eʃən] 處境，境遇

同義詞：circumstances, state of affairs

相關詞：no-win situation 絕無成功可能的局面；situation analysis 現狀分析法

⊘ **respect** *v. n.* [rɪ`spɛkt] 敬重，尊敬，方面

同義詞：adore, value, appreciate

相關詞：in all respects 從各方面看來；respect oneself 自重

⊘ **regretfully** *adv.* [rɪ`grɛtfəlɪ] 抱歉地

同義詞：sorrowfully, remorsefully

相關詞：to say regretfully 遺憾地說

⊘ **leave a message** *ph.* 留言

同義詞：leave word, leave a note

關鍵句型

be trying to coordinate with Sb.　正嘗試與某人協調…

例句說明：

· The management **is trying to coordinate with** the labor regarding the raise rate of salary.
管理層正試著與勞工協調調薪幅度事宜。

Sb. have no choice but to ...　某人不得不

例句說明：

· We **have no choice but to** return the damaged lots.
我們沒有別的選擇，不得不退回這批損壞的貨。

Sb. be occupied with ...　某人正忙於…

例句說明：

· John **is occupied with** translating an English report.
約翰正忙著翻譯一份英文報告。

Sb. be obliged to ...　某人不得不…

例句說明：

· **I was obliged to** abandon this business.
我不得不放棄這筆交易。

英文書信這樣寫

Request of Order Cancellation 取消訂單

Dear Tony,

I have to notify you that we are cancelling our P/O No. 7788, as we can't accept such a long postponement.

The delay of the goods has caused great loss to our business. In accordance with the terms of our contract, we are obtaining the rights to ask for compensation due to the delay over two weeks.

Shall there be any questions, please let me know.

Sincerely yours,
Tom Smith

— 中文翻譯 —

湯尼 您好：

我在此通知貴司，我司將取消第7788號訂單事宜，我們無法接受長時間延遲交貨。

貨物的延遲已對我司業務造成極大的損失。依據雙方合約條款，延遲逾兩週以上，我司將有權請求賠償。

如有任何疑問，請讓我知悉。

湯姆 史密斯 敬啟

知識補給

　　未交貨訂單（**Back Order**），又稱「手頭訂單」，是製造商在特定時期，如歲末年終時在手未完成的訂單。持有部分的未交貨訂單為製造商經營必然會面臨的問題，然而若未交貨訂單過多，則表示交貨時間太長，將衍伸出客戶轉單的風險；反之，若未交貨訂單過少，則表示銷售量下降，生產提前結束，導致後續產能過剩。

　　收到客戶訂單到完成交貨所需的時間即為所謂的「交貨期限」。交貨期限的長短其實也反映出經濟情勢，當經濟不景氣，新訂單量會稅減，相對的，後續未交貨訂單也會減少，交貨期限就會縮短；當景氣佳，新訂單訊速增加，未交貨訂單也會持續累積，因此交貨期限也會拉長。

Notes 筆記欄

賣方賠償
Make Compensation

國貿關鍵字 ｜ 國貿賠償規則 ｜

　　國貿賠償常見情況有以下 ：1.信用不佳：因交易對手信用不佳，不確實覆行契約義務，導致另一方遭受損害而提出索賠，這是最常見的索賠原因2.語言文字不同（溝通落差）3.不可抗力事故：例如因天災致無法如期交貨，或因政策法令變動而無法順利匯出貨款，只要契約中有訂明不可抗力事故條款，這類索賠通常較易解決。

情境說明

Buyer urges seller to compensate the loss caused by packaging error.

買方公司要求賣方公司賠償因錯誤包裝導致的損失。

角色介紹

買方｜Buyer: B, ABC Co., Ltd.

賣方｜Seller: S, Best International Trade Corp.

情境對話

B: Hello, Tony. This is Tom Smith calling from ABC Co.

B：你好，湯尼，我是ABC公司的湯姆 史密斯。

S: What's on your mind, Tom?

S：有什麼事嗎，湯姆？

B: I'm calling to discuss about our compensation request for our P/O No. 9900 with mislabeling.

B：我打來是要討論有關我們第9900號訂單標籤錯誤的賠償。

S: <u>As I mentioned earlier,</u> we haven't come up with a decision to entertain your claim.

B: <u>Concerning</u> the backlog of orders we can't deal with, <u>we believe</u> the compensation amount is quite reasonable.

S: We'll need to have our internal discussion.

B: I hope that you would let me know the result before this Wednesday.

S：如同我先前陳述的，我司仍未決定接受您的索賠條件。

B：對於不能處理積壓的訂單，我司認為這是相當合理的賠償金額。

S：我司將必須進行內部討論。

B：希望您能讓我在這個星期三前知道結果。

Buyer requests seller to extend the time limit of a claim.

買方公司要求賣方公司延長索賠期限。

角色介紹

買方｜Buyer: B, ABC Co., Ltd.

賣方｜Seller: S, Best International Trade Corp.

情境對話

B: Hello, Tony. This is Tom Smith calling from ABC Co.

B：你好，湯尼，我是ABC公司的湯姆 史密斯。

S: What's on your mind, Tom?

S：有什麼事嗎，湯姆？

B: I'm pleased to confirm with you that the shipment against our P/O No. 2323 had duly arrived at the destination.

B：很高興向您確認我司第2323號訂單已準時抵達目的地。

S: Great to hear that.

S：很高興聽到這個消息。

B: Well. There's one thing I want to ask a favor of you.

B：是這樣的，有一件事我想請您幫個忙。

S: Please go ahead.

S：請說吧。

B: The recent strike at the Port of London has delayed the unloading and inspection.

B：最近在倫敦港口的罷工事件已延遲了卸貨和檢查。

S: Yeah, I've just heard about the news.

B: Per the contract, we're requested to raise any claim within 30 days from the arrival date of the shipment. We'd like to request an extension of the time limit for the claim on the above shipment to 45 days.

S: OK. That shouldn't be a problem.

S：是的，我剛已聽說這個消息了。

B：根據合約，任何索賠要求須在到貨日算起的30天內提出，我司想要求將上述貨物的索賠期限延長到45天。

S：好吧，這應該不是問題。

關鍵字彙

⊘ **continue** v. [kənˋtɪnjʊ] 繼續，持續

同義詞：last, to go on with, keep

相關詞：continue arguing 持續爭論；continue to develop 持續發展

⊘ **come up with** ph. 想出

同義詞：eventuate, work out, figure out

相關詞：come out with 發表，說出

⊘ **backlog** n. [ˋbækˌlɔg] 積壓，存貨

同義詞：reserve, stockpile

相關詞：backlog of work 積壓的工作；a backlog of flight 航班滯留

⊘ **conclusion** n. [kənˋkluʒən] 結論，結果

同義詞：result, settlement

相關詞：in conclusion 最後；jump to conclusions 過早下結論

⊘ **compensation amount** *ph.* 賠償金額

同義詞：repayment value, reimbursement figure

相關詞：compensation fund 補償基金

⊘ **strike** *n.* [straɪk] 罷工

同義詞：down tools, walk off the job

相關詞：student's strike 罷課；prolonged strike 長期罷工

⊘ **unload** *v.* [ʌn`lod] 卸貨

同義詞：discharge, unpack

相關詞：loading and unloading 裝卸貨；unloading port 卸貨港

⊘ **extension** *n.* [ɪk`stɛnʃən] 延長

同義詞：postponement, prolongation, continuation

相關詞：extension line 分機；extension cord 延長線

⊘ **go ahead** *ph.* 繼續

同義詞：go on, continue

相關詞：Keep going! Go!, Forward! 前進吧！

關鍵句型

As Sb. mentioned earlier, ... 　如某人先前所說

例句說明：

· **As he mentioned earlier,** the business has raised up this month.

如他先前所說，本月業績飛漲。

· **As I mentioned earlier,** our offer is quite favorable.

如我先前所說，我司的報價相當優惠。

Concerning Sth., Sb. believe... 　對於某事，某人認為⋯

例句說明：

· **Concerning** the ingredient to get promotion, my supervisor **believes** that ability is prior to seniority.

對於晉升的要素，主管認為能力重於年資。

· **Concerning** the future of our company, the management **believes** that business development is the key point.

對於我們的公司的未來，管理層認為關鍵在於業務開發。

Sb. be pleased to confirm that ... 　某人很高興確認⋯

例句說明：

· **The assistant manager is pleased to confirm that** our team's performance meets and exceeds the target this month.

副理很高興的確認我們的部門本月業績達成且超過目標。

英文書信這樣寫

Extend the Time Limit of Claim 延期索賠

Dear Tom,

Please accept our sincere apology for not replying to your claim request promptly, as I have been preparing for the quality meeting to discuss the functionality problem raised by you.

Therefore, please grant us more days to work out the solution and extend the time limit of the claim to the end of this month.

Please feel free to let me know if you have any concern.

Sincerely yours,
Tony Yang

— 中文翻譯 —

湯姆 您好：

很抱歉未能及時回覆貴司的索賠請求，因我還在忙著準備品質會議討論貴司提出的功能異常問題。

因此，請給我多幾天找出解決方案，並請延長索賠期限至本月底。

如貴司有任何考量，請不吝告知。

湯尼 楊 敬啟